JAIME GOICOECHEA ZÚÑIGA

SURREAL MÉXICO

BOOK I:
THE LAW OF THE MEXICAN

Surreal Mexico

Book I:
The Law of the Mexican

Jaime Goicoechea Zúñiga

Style correction and layout: Javier Torras de Ugarte.
Translated by Lawrence Baker:
 lawrencejbaker1997@outlook.com

'In no way will I return to Mexico; I cannot stand being in a country more surreal than my paintings.'

Salvador Dalí.

'Do not try to understand Mexico through reason; you will have better luck from the absurd, Mexico is the most surreal country in the world.'

André Breton.

Table of Contents

Prologue. Surreal Mexico: Connected Stories.

In the pages that now unfold before you, the embrace of the unusual and mysterious awaits. Step into Surreal Mexico, a literary world where the border between the real and the fantastical fades, and intertwined stories create a hypnotic tapestry that will enthrall you. Here, tales intersect like underground currents, weaving a web of intrigue and wonder that reveals the astonishing richness of the human experience.

This journey immerses us in the lives of disparate characters, whose adversities take shape in juxtaposed short stories, all connected by subtle threads that weave a unique literary tapestry. Surreal Mexico is not just a collection of stories but a mosaic of perspectives that plunges you into the emotional depths of each protagonist. Their struggles and triumphs unfold before you like a fan of vibrant emotions: pain clashes with joy, sadness with love, violence with tradition.

The author challenges literary boundaries with a style both dazzling and original. With skill, he injects metaphors and symbolism into every line. The interconnecting nature of the stories is the soul of this surreal world. Through clever twists and unexpected revelations, characters and plots intersect, revealing that their destinies are inextricably linked. Surreal Mexico is an invitation to explore the depths of our shared humanity, reminding us that, though our lives may seem isolated, we are actually part of an invisible web.

Thus, this literary journey immerses us in the most intimate aspects of the human experience, where the real and the imaginary coexist. It reveals that magic can hide in the simplest of details, and that every moment can contain the seed of the extraordinary.

Prepare to dive into this unique journey, where the ordinary meets the extraordinary, and the playful blends with the profound. Welcome to Agua Fría, Puebla, where the doors to the unimaginable are about to open. Step forward, explorer, and delve into this literary labyrinth. Let yourself be enveloped by the wonder and surprise that only words can offer.

The Law of the Mexican

Cirilo Flores was riding at a leisurely pace towards the picturesque village of Agua Fría, atop his faithful donkey, when a vivid memory from the past stole up on him with force: his childhood, that indelible day when his father took him to the riverbank to catch crayfish. In that instant, ancestral knowledge etched itself into his memory; the art of snaring these creatures revealed its splendor when the waters swelled and roiled. The image of his father, enveloped in life's simplicity, holding two cone-shaped traps woven from vines, was imprinted on his consciousness. Cirilo, intoxicated by anticipation, felt touched by the grace of being summoned by his father. Together, they journeyed for twenty minutes, following an unspoken pact, until they reached the river.

Juan Flores, Cirilo's father, embodied the serenity of one who preferred to communicate through eloquent actions and silences, magnifying the worth of every connection between them. In the waters of the Tepetate River, they wove the network of their traps, set defiantly against the current, waiting for the crayfish. After arranging the traps, they embarked on the journey back home, only to return later and find the traps brimming with their catch, the juicy treasures of nature. It was then that Cirilo's mother, the bearer of culinary magic, conjured the crayfish huatape, Cirilo's favorite dish. In a sensory feast, the nourishing broth intertwined with masa, guajillo chilies, the heat of piquin chilies, and the aroma of epazote. And so, on that day, Cirilo surrendered to the communion with his palate, savoring

13

not one but three servings of the tasty delicacy that connected him to his roots.

That seemingly trivial experience had become a treasure he housed within him like a sacred relic. Every time he rode through the pathways of his memory, the murmur of the Tepetate's waters intertwined with his father's love, woven in the gentle swaying of the vine traps. And so, as the river and the crayfish danced in his mind, Cirilo continued his journey towards Agua Fría.

Time flowed like the water of an unceasing river, carrying Cirilo's memories in its relentless current. With the passage of years, Cirilo's challenging circumstances formed a backdrop of nostalgia, against which golden images of moments past were projected. Old age, silent and patient, had arrived at his doorstep, leaving indelible marks on his body and soul.

The weathering of time manifested in the nervous tic that danced in his hands, a constant reminder of his battle in the California fields, where he had toiled with poisons of pesticides. Rheumatoid arthritis, like a ravenous wolf, had taken hold of his waist and back, weaving pain into every corner of his being. This constant discomfort stood immutable as a mountain, robbing him of the possibility of maintaining consistent employment. In the familiarity of Agua Fría, the kindness and charity of the locals were his crutches. Always ready to extend a hand to those in need, they constituted Cirilo's sanctuary. However, at times, an unpleasant echo emerged from among them. A malicious shadow, harsh in tone, hurling hurtful insults: 'Go to the wilderness, there you won't lack food!'

The surroundings of Agua Fría unfurled like a lush garden, offering a multicolored feast of fruit trees: ripe mangoes like suns, soursops guarding secrets beneath their wrinkled skin, tamarinds bittersweet as memory, bananas curving into arcs of sweetness, papayas unraveling their flavor in a burst of juiciness, avocados with their hidden richness, radiant oranges like daybreak, and sapotes evoking an embrace of the earth. However, in life's paradoxical way, Cirilo's appetite did not stir for fruits. His teeth, victims of relentless time, refused their duty. The longing for meat, a yearning rooted deep within his being, beckoned to his senses. Despite his lack of teeth, his desire was indomitable, and the longing for the taste and texture of meat accompanied him every step of his journey, like a constant echo of the passion still burning within him.

The hunting and fishing skills that were once his pastime and livelihood were now beyond him due to the chronic pain nested in his back. The ancient paths through the jungle and along the riverbanks, where he had pursued prey and skillfully cast nets, were closed to him like doors sealed by unyielding fate. Every movement became a dance of agony, and pain stood as a fierce guardian, preventing him from indulging in the pleasures he had once known.

However, amidst the desolation, a friendly figure emerged, bringing solace to his lonely heart. His faithful donkey, christened with the name Donkey-xote, a wordplay that echoed from his memories of distant lands in California, stood as an unwavering confidant. That the donkey could not speak was not a barrier; Cirilo talked to Donkey-xote for hours, sharing thoughts and emotions he couldn't express elsewhere. In the silent echo of these conversations, he found relief and the feeling that somehow his voice was heard.

His bond with the donkey transcended words. Every caress and shared glance held a deep complicity, as if both understood each other's secrets without the need for explanations. Donkeyjote became much more than mere companionship; he embodied the family Cirilo had lost and the strength that sustained him. Every morning, as the sun painted the horizon with warm colors, Cirilo and Donkey-xote set off on their daily journey to the post office. Cirilo's anticipation of Mr. Smith's correspondence, an eagerness undiminished by time, drove them forward on familiar paths.

For Cirilo, the steady approach of the donkey on the dusty road transformed into a symbol of perseverance and hope. In its hooves, the echo of past and future resonated like a heartbeat. And so, in each step, in every breeze that caressed their faces, Cirilo and Donkey-xote wove a silent narrative, an indomitable bond that kept them united in the face of adversity and loneliness.

Cirilo had built his home on the outskirts of Agua Fría, on a corner that, though modest, overflowed with homeyness. His house, a pile of weathered wood clinging to the hillside as if it had grown organically from the earth itself.

The generosity of a charitable soul had granted him this roof, a gift that allowed him to navigate the abyss of destitution. Without that outstretched hand, his existence would have been completely at the mercy of life's inclemencies and whims. The house was flanked by a well of crystal-clear water, a vital source that brought relief from thirst and the oppressive heat. Beside it, a sour orange tree extended its branches like protective arms, weaving a pleasant canopy that became Donkey-xote's refuge. The donkey, faithful and patient, shared his life with Cirilo, and under the sour orange tree's shade, the bond between man and beast blossomed in the shared stillness of their days.

At the rear of the dwelling, a gift of love and solidarity rose in the form of a maize field. A tangible display of the empathy the small town had for Cirilo. However, the weakness of his body, wracked by pain and arthritis, prevented him from tending to the plants. The crows, cunning and hungry, found in the field a pantry they devoured voraciously, leaving stripped and withered stalks in their wake.

The natural gardens around the house offered a palette of bright colors. Wildflowers raised their heads toward the sun like small flames in a world dominated by shadows. Beyond these paths of beauty lay four graves, marking a corner of the garden that Cirilo visited with devotion. One large cross and three small ones were the silent witnesses of a past that accompanied him in the present. Once every year, Cirilo knelt, a silent prayer on his lips, and cleaned each cross with a love that transcended words.

Every corner of that modest home harbored fragments of a man's story, a blend of struggles, sacrifices, and moments shared with a donkey and a handful of compassionate souls. The silent walls and the whispering wind held his narrative, each year of weather on the wood was a chapter written in the book of his life. Agua Fría, with its compassion and shadows, bore witness to Cirilo's journey, a man who had faced adversity and built his own refuge amidst the dust and heat.

In the heart of the bustling market of Agua Fría, where colors and scents converged in a symphony of life, Cirilo ventured with his faithful companion. He tied Donkey-xote to a lamppost and the donkey stood, an anchor of patience amidst the frenetic swirl of the market. Lowering his gaze, Cirilo spotted a forgotten coin on the ground, a relic of spent value that seemed to have been abandoned by time. The dull metal, once a symbol of wealth, lay in the palm of his hand like a reminder of life's changing nature.

Coin in hand, Cirilo approached the tomato vendor, a man whose wrinkles spoke of years working in the fields. The coin, though stripped of its former power, still carried the weight of its history. Out of compassion and empathy, the tomato vendor gifted him a shining red tomato, as bright as if the fruit bore the reflection of a scorching sun. Cirilo received it with gratitude and reverence, stowing it in his knapsack with the care one bestows upon a treasure.

Continuing his journey through the market, the aromas became a sensory festival, inviting him to indulge in the culinary pleasures laid out before him. The irresistible scent of molotes frying in lard wafted through the air, tempting him with their golden and crispy flavor. However, his empty pockets reminded him of the harsh reality of his situation. Nevertheless, he couldn't resist stopping and drinking in the aroma that filled the air, allowing himself a brief moment of indulgence in the fantasy of flavors his palate longed for.

Destiny led him to the zacahuil stand, where giant tamales filled with succulent pork, corn masa, and intoxicating spices seemed like a dream come true. Hunger, his constant companion, roared into life. The temptation was immense, and the desire to sink his teeth into that delicacy felt uncontrollable. But once again, the empty wallet held him back. He forced his trembling hands to grip his knapsack tighter so that no one would see them shake.

The market continued its dance, a choreography of commerce and human relationships. Cirilo carried on, one man amidst the crowd, bearing not only the burden of his hunger but also the weight of his history. He crossed paths with Chelito, a master of the culinary arts who excelled in cooking pork carnitas in a copper pot. The golden aroma wafted through the air like a melody that stirred the hunger of everyone it touched. Cirilo's eyes filled with desire, while his absent teeth ached with nostalgia. He walked on.

His journey took him to Don Froylán's store, a point on the path where debt had become a knot of concern. The pending sum weighed on his conscience, a burden his empty pocket couldn't alleviate. His strategy was simple: circumnavigate the store and keep a distance from the man to whom he owed the debt. However, every step he took merely held the inevitable at bay, an encounter he could only postpone but not evade.

Cirilo found refuge in Doña María's medicinal herbs stand. The elderly woman possessed the knowledge of healing plants, a treasure passed down through generations. Each visit was a ritual of relief, where Doña María kindly provided him with herbs that brought momentary relief to his back pain. The woman's wrinkled hands caressed the leaves with devotion, as if each plant carried the ancestral secrets of healing. And Cirilo, grateful, received the herbs with humility, knowing that his frail body depended on these gifts of nature.

Thus, the market became a stage of contrasts, where temptations and limitations coexisted. Cirilo continued his journey, a soul in search of sustenance and solace, surrounded by stories and aromas that wove the fabric of life in Agua Fría. Every step was a struggle, a reminder of his resilience in the face of difficulties, and a celebration of the small joys that could still be found amidst adversity. And as the market continued its dance, Cirilo shuffled on, carrying with him the burdens and gifts that life bestowed on him in his daily journey.

As he reached the edge of the market, Cirilo crossed paths with the town bullies, those who reveled in others' misery and found satisfaction in humiliation. They approached with false friendliness, extending an invitation to share some cecina tacos, knowing well that the result would be a spectacle of laughter at his expense. The cecina, dry and tough, was an impossible challenge for his worn teeth, and each attempt to chew it was an act of perseverance in the face of ridicule. The bullies laughed heartily, as if each bite were a source of hilarity greater than the last. The air was full of their cruel laughter, and Cirilo, once again, bore silently the humiliation and contempt they cast upon him.

After these bitter interactions, Cirilo headed to the post office. The long absence of correspondence from Mr. Smith loomed as an echo of silence, a shadow that darkened his expectations. He wondered if the old friend was still among the living. Uncertainty weighed on his shoulders as he inquired about any mail.

However, in Cirilo's heart, hope still flickered, a fragile flame that refused to go out. Each visit to the post office was an act of faith, a reminder that connections to the past could be kept alive through ink and paper. Although Mr. Smith's words had not arrived on this occasion, Cirilo did not allow himself to give in to uncertainty. He left the post office with resignation, but nevertheless resolved to keep waiting, to keep hope alive amidst adversity.

The sky, once clear, had given way to clouds that cast a gray and humid mantle over Agua Fría. Donkey-xote's footsteps echoed on the cobbled street as Cirilo made his way back home. The air was thick with moisture, and his ragged shirt clung to his skin. The daytime heat was beginning to yield to a cooler afternoon, yet the oppressive atmosphere remained.

As Cirilo rode, the sound of chants and prayers began to fill the humid air. A procession was approaching, a torrent of fervor and devotion that blocked the streets and disrupted the town's usual course. Cirilo, with no choice but to stop, watched as hundreds of people moved in unison, following the figure of the

Virgin of the Dump. The scene was overwhelming, a display of collective faith enveloping everyone in its path.

The procession carried memories of the past, and Cirilo couldn't help but recall the day when the Virgin of the Dump had defended him, even challenging the leader of the town bullies. Her words echoed in his mind: 'If they were beating you, I would defend you too.' Her courage had left an indelible impression on his memory, a display of compassion and justice that transcended circumstances.

Once, to Cirilo, the Virgin of the Dump had been Felipa, a young woman who lived at the municipal waste disposal center, in a small oasis carved out from amidst the trash. Her life was a testament to perseverance and resilience, a reminder that beauty and dignity could flourish even in the most unlikely places. However, over time, the fame of the Virgin of the Dump had grown, and thousands of people now came to receive her blessing and experience the peace her presence bestowed.

Swept up in the procession and the chanting, Cirilo for a moment felt part of something greater, a community united by faith and hope. Although his life was marked by adversity, he found solace in moments like this, where shared devotion brightened the monotony of his existence. The sun disappeared behind the gray clouds, and the procession continued its path, carrying with it a sense of connection and transcendence that crossed the boundaries of time and space.

On the outskirts of Agua Fría, the first raindrops began to fall, whispers from the sky that foreshadowed the imminent storm. Cirilo felt the air cooling, and a shiver ran down his spine. He knew he had to hurry if he didn't want to get caught in the rain. As he went on along the path, the trails he had known since childhood became increasingly blurred under the rain's advancing veil.

He stopped at the threshold of the forest, where the landscape changed radically. Rolling hills stretched before him, covered in vegetation that grew greener with each raindrop. The scent of wet earth and fresh grass filled his senses, and the subtle whisper of the wind spoke of secrets that only nature could share.

His eyes settled on the town cemetery, a place where time seemed to have left its mark with unyielding cruelty. The crosses, faded and worn, lay in eternal silence, marking the lives of those bodies that dwelt now below the earth. It was a place forgotten by many, a corner of Agua Fría that seemed to have fallen into the abyss.

Despite the unsettling feeling that this place evoked, Cirilo knew he had no other option. He closed his eyes and advanced, each step resonating with the echo of the silent stories of the lives beneath his feet. The rain intensified, soaking him and reminding him of the many times he had sought refuge in the abandoned house that stood at the heart of the cemetery.

As he crossed that place of eternal rest, his mind wandered. He thought of the lives that had passed, of the loves and pains they had experienced. He wondered if someone, someday, would walk here thinking about their own story, about their struggle to survive and find meaning amidst difficulties. The rain had turned the path to mud, and every step was a challenge. However, Cirilo pressed on. The smell of wet earth filled the air.

The wind whispered in a melancholic lament as Cirilo advanced, and somewhere in the branches of the dripping trees a bird called mournfully. Every step he took resonated in the silence, like an intimate dance with the forest and the rainy sky.

His thoughts intertwined with the beating of his heart, each one laden with the sorrows and aspirations that had shaped his life.

The mystery of the mourning bird intrigued him, but his mind was overwhelmed by other concerns when suddenly a figure on a jet-black horse appeared on the path ahead, a specter of darkness that seemed to have emerged from the very shadows of his soul. Although he couldn't see the figure's eyes, he felt its penetrating gaze, as if it were reading his deepest thoughts, as if it knew every corner of his being.

'Why did it take you so long to come for me?' Cirilo said in a sarcastic tone.

Cirilo was exhausted. He had become a man tired of fighting, of facing each day with the certainty that pain and misery would accompany him until the end. Life seemed to have become an insufferable burden, and the idea of leaving it behind was now his only relief.

A glimmer of an idea crossed his mind as he gazed at the headstones. A final act of defiance, an attempt to wrest control of his destiny from the dark figure on the horse. However, the decision was neither impulsive nor hasty; it was a deep reflection on his own existence, on the ups and downs that had marked his path.

On the precipice between life and death, Cirilo found a moment of clarity. He remembered the taste of acamaya stew, the serene look of Donkey-xote, the procession of the Virgin of the Dump, and the stories buried in the cemetery. He clung to these fragments of beauty amidst the darkness. The wind seemed to whisper a message of resistance.

She, shrouded in an aura of the ethereal, dismounted from the jet-black horse with an elegance and solemnity that contrasted with the scythe she held in her hand. The blade gleamed like a dark promise, a symbol of the inevitable transition that everyone faces at some point. Cirilo looked at her without fear; his gaze was like a deep well of serenity in which the darkness of the scythe seemed to fade away.

The harvester of souls was accustomed to encountering looks of terror, to hearing desperate pleas, and seeing people struggle for one last breath of life. But Cirilo was different; his eyes did not reflect despair or fear, but rather steady acceptance and serenity. The calmness that emanated from him was like a refreshing breeze on a sweltering day.

The distant sound of children laughing and splashing in the nearby river painted a vivid contrast with the scene unfolding in that place. Life continued its course amidst the contemplation of death. That chorus of children sounded like a song of hope, a melody that seemed to defy the darkness itself.

Cirilo's words, spoken with resigned determination, echoed in the air, filling the space between them with a brave acceptance of the inevitable. The figure in front of him seemed to pause, as if her ears had caught something not in the present but in a future yet to come.

In an instant, the sound of the horse's trot echoed against the headstones, breaking the silence that had fallen like a veil. The animal quickly moved away, heading toward where the children played and laughed without a care in the world. The sound of hooves faded, leaving behind its echo in Cirilo's mind.

The figure turned her gaze toward the same horizon the horse had headed for. It seemed that something beyond what Cirilo could see had captured her attention. A glimpse of understanding crossed Cirilo's mind, a glimpse of what had happened. The harvester of souls had chosen not to take Cirilo at that moment. Perhaps she had felt the strength of his determination, the acceptance of the inevitable, and the peace he had found amidst his suffering.

The figure on the horse was not just a messenger of death; she was also a silent witness to life continuing, even in the darkest moments. With her departure, she had left a message in the wind: life and death were intertwined, and in that delicate balance, Cirilo had found a place to rest his weary heart.

Thus, with the echo of children's laughter still present in the air, Cirilo resumed his journey home. Each step was a reminder of his own strength and of the beauty that still existed in his world. Despite the shadows that had surrounded him, he had found a glimmer of light within himself. And as the clouds slowly parted, allowing the golden rays of the sun to filter through, Cirilo knew that there was still more to discover on the path ahead of him.

The next day, the clouds hung heavy in the sky, silent witnesses to the grief that enveloped Agua Fría. The air was laden with sadness, and the market, usually a bustling and lively place, seemed to have fallen into a respectful silence for the fate of the four children.

Cirilo, with his heart torn to pieces, walked through the market as if carrying the weight of the world on his shoulders. Each step resonated like an echo of his own sorrow, a melancholic cadence that seemed to merge with the weeping of the clouds. The news of the tragedy had spread quickly through the town, and curious eyes rested on Cirilo as he moved forward, not fully understanding his pain.

Regret pulsed in his chest, a discordant beat that hammered in his mind again and again. The harvester of souls, who had come so close to him, seemed to have taken a different path, one that had claimed young and innocent lives. The irony haunted him: why had he, a man on the brink of the abyss, still continued in this world, while those children full of life had been torn from it?

The emotion contained within him finally exploded, and Cirilo fell to his knees. His tears mixed with the raindrops falling from the sky, as if the heavens themselves shared in his grief. Sobs escaped from his throat in a deep lament, a cry of pain and despair that seemed to resonate throughout every market.

'Why did you take them?' his voice rose in a distressed cry, a cry that seemed directed toward the very heavens themselves. 'Why didn't you take me instead? I'm worthless, I don't deserve to live, they were children with their whole lives ahead of them!'

The gazes of those present were fixed upon him in a mixture of bewilderment and compassion. Some murmured among themselves, questioning his sanity, while others simply watched in silence, perhaps understanding the depth of his pain.

When he finally managed to control his tears, he stood up with painful effort. He mounted Donkey-xote and ventured into the streets of Agua Fría, the rain soaking his clothes and making his back ache. But nothing mattered anymore. His physical pain merged with his emotional agony, and his soul seemed immersed in darkness.

The streets were deserted, as if the town itself shared in his grief. The rain fell incessantly, like tears from the sky that joined Cirilo's tears. His donkey followed the path without instruction from Cirilo.

Sadness enveloped him like a heavy blanket, and as he rode through the town that had been his home, the loss of those innocent children echoed within him. He had lost track of time and space; his mind a whirlwind of pain and guilt.

In the midst of that internal storm, a truth forced its way through: Cirilo was not only dealing with his own suffering but also with the burden of those he loved and had lost. His pain had become a reflection of Agua Fría's collective sadness, a sadness that clung to every corner of the town like a persistent shadow.

As he rode on, his mind became a labyrinth of unanswered questions, of guilt without redemption. The rain continued to fall, like a shared lament between the sky and the earth. And in the midst of that rain, in the midst of that shared pain, Cirilo longed to find a ray of hope, a way to redeem his own suffering and that of those who had departed too soon. In his desperation, Cirilo longed to see once again the dark horse and rider, to ask her to help him understand the cruel fate that had taken the innocent children.

No sooner had the thought occurred to him than he found her, mounted on her horse, standing in front of a cantina. She appeared before him as an impenetrable figure, indifferent to human compassion. Cirilo clung to her leg, demanding: 'Why did you take them? Why didn't you take me instead?'

Her response was an act of disdain and rejection, a cold gesture that left Cirilo even more crushed. The embrace he sought to find in her became a ruthless blow, a kick that sent him rolling on the ground like a puppet whose strings had just been cut. The mark of her spur on his cheek was like a symbol of his encounter with the inevitable reality: Death does not heed pleas or supplications. She dismounted from the horse and strode into the cantina.

Inside the cantina, the violence that ruled in that place sparked into flame. Gunshots echoed like a sad symphony of self-destruction, claiming the lives of three more people. Cirilo, still on the ground, became a silent witness to the tragedy that followed Death wherever she went. The figure in her black charro had become a catalyst for chaos and desolation.

Dust mixed with the bitter taste of his own helplessness as he lay on the ground. The world around him seemed to fade into a gloomy haze, as if he were trapped in a waking dream. Amidst the chaos, one question persisted in his mind: why was he still alive while others were mercilessly exterminated? As he lay there, he heard the clink of her spurs, the swish of her cloak as she mounted her horse.

The echo of the gunshots faded, leaving behind a silence heavy with meaning. Cirilo slowly got up, his bones protesting the effort. His gaze turned toward the horizon, where Death had vanished, like a shadow dissolving into darkness.

His thoughts swirled in his mind. Sadness for the lost children mixed with the fear of what Death held for him, and the incomprehension of destiny assaulted him from all angles. But amid the confusion and pain, a determination began to sprout. The figure of Death was fading on the horizon, but Cirilo's story was far from over.

The days slipped by like gray shadows, laden with despair and desolation. Cirilo's house, once a refuge, had turned into a prison of sadness; the very walls seemed to close in on him with every somber thought. Physical pain intertwined with emotional torment, forming an inextricable amalgam that prevented him from finding even a glimmer of relief. His weathered face and the deep dark circles beneath his eyes were a faithful reflection of his inner state. Nights, once a pause for rest, had become endless bouts of insomnia. Dreams were momentary refuges that slipped away upon awakening, leaving him anchored in the very reality he was desperate to escape.

Nature itself seemed to mirror his torment. The voracious crows perched overlooking his cornfield, hungry and defiant. Their claws ripping loose the ripe heads of corn was a cruel metaphor for how adversity loomed over him, devouring his hopes and his attempts to overcome the darkness. He had no strength to confront them, to defend what remained of his food.

However, amid the storm, something began to emerge. A spark, faint as a distant glimmer, flickered within him. It was the seed of resistance, the germ of the strength dormant deep within his being. With each day of despair, with each night of insomnia, that spark grew, fueled by the will to find a ray of light amid the penumbra.

Cirilo found himself at a crossroads between resignation and struggle. Although his strength was depleted, and the path to recovery seemed steep and arduous, there was something in him that refused to give up. He clung to that spark, to the small promise that there was something beyond the sadness. Even though the days remained grim, Cirilo was willing to seek the light, even if it meant confronting the darkness.

The next day, Cirilo mounted Donkey-xote and headed to the hill near his home, where there grew a tree surrounded by thick grass half a meter high. As he climbed the hill, he saw Death sitting on a rock, sharpening her scythe. 'This is a good omen!' he exclaimed with a wry smile.

The hill seemed to be the stage for a macabre dance between life and death, where Cirilo struggled between two divergent destinations. The hill, a silent witness to his misfortunes, stood as a symbol of the duality within him: the struggle for survival and the fatal attraction to the abyss.

The figure of Death, calmly sharpening her scythe, seemed to weave the thread of destiny with inexorable patience. Her presence in that place resonated like a mysterious echo, as if she were an enigmatic guide that stood in the way of Cirilo's attempts to escape suffering. However, this time, the shadowy smile on her lips seemed to offer a different nuance.

He reached the top of the hill, took out a rope, threw it over one of the branches of the lone tree, then tied one end to the tree trunk and knotted the other around his neck. He climbed onto Donkey-xote and let himself hang. The rope obstructed his breathing, and his body hung for a few seconds.

The hill was a stage of liberation and torment, a duality that was reflected in Cirilo's final act. The rope, a symbol of his desire to escape the chains of pain, turned into a deadly trap that severed his breath. In those moments of suspension, the struggle for life was palpable, even as it intertwined with the shadow of the end.

But Death herself added an unpredictable twist to the tragedy. The scythe, once a symbol of doom, became a liberating instrument. The cutting of the rope marked a rupture in the narrative, a moment where life and death intertwined inextricably. Cirilo fell, his body hitting the ground with a cry of pain and frustration.

The cry that emanated from Cirilo as he caught his breath was a heart-wrenching lament, an expression of powerlessness in the face of his own situation. The failed act confronted him with the reality that even in his attempt to escape suffering, he remained trapped in a cycle of pain and abandonment. The departure of Death, once again, reminded him of his loneliness, as if not even the final destination wanted to embrace him.

That night, Cirilo sat outside his house, gazing at the stars and the full moon, and Death visited him again. She maintained a distance, neither too far nor too close. In the stillness of the starry night, Cirilo's figure stood out like a solitary guardian of his own reflections. While he watched, Death danced amid the darkness, her fingers tracing ethereal figures in the air, as if the cosmos itself had joined her rhythm, with the stars as her stage and the moon as her sole witness. The jet-black horse gleamed in the moonlight, a creature of shadows and mysteries. The horse's saddle and the intricacies of the lariat's design resonated like ancestral melodies, intertwining Death's skills as a charro with the cosmic dance of the stars.

On the threshold of the night, amid whispers to the stars, Cirilo spoke to the wind. His words resonated with a blend of admiration and questioning, as if he were speaking with the cosmos itself. Cirilo's voice, murmuring in the silence of the night, seemed like an invitation to a debate with the incomprehensible.

'We may be unique in the universe, but here on Earth, we are all the same,' he murmured. 'Death, you are both beautiful and severe with me, dual, impartial, and yet unjust with all. You take whomever you please, deserving or not. Like a game of chance, no one knows what life holds. What is your purpose? You confound us humans. You ignore me, ready to depart, and take those who wish to stay. I know that someday you'll come for me, and I'll be here waiting. My patience is greater than your generosity.'

His words shed light on the enigma of life and death, as if he were trying to unravel the designs of an indifferent universe. Death, as she danced, seemed to listen attentively to each of his words, as if time itself had stopped to witness that moment of introspection. The night, turned into a confidant, absorbed every thought and every sigh, creating a fragile bond between Cirilo and Death.

Thus, under the gaze of the stars and the moon, the conversation between Cirilo and Death continued, weaving unanswered questions and reflections that got lost in the vastness of the night sky.

When morning came, Cirilo was plunged into a dark tunnel of despair, a place where time seemed to have stopped, and the shadows of his sadness enveloped him like a leaden cloak. Days passed like ghosts. The walls of his house seemed to close in once more, and the sun, once a symbol of hope and vitality, became a distant specter whose touch he barely felt.

He woke at twilight, his circadian rhythms had reversed in an attempt to escape the pain that gripped his heart. Nights bore witness to his exhausting battle against sorrow, while days dissolved into unchanging lethargy. Loneliness was his constant companion, and the walls of his home seemed to guard the echoes of his suffering.

In the midst of this desolation, a flash of clarity broke through his mind. A daring thought, almost like a lightning bolt in the darkness, penetrated his consciousness. Since Death had foiled his plan to end his life at his own hands, perhaps he could provoke the town bullies by challenging their authority and daring to confront them with sharp words. Perhaps, in an act of recklessness, he could draw their violence upon himself and put an end to his suffering once and for all.

This plan revived a glimmer of determination in his heart. For a moment, he felt like he had control over his destiny, that he could make a bold decision in a world that seemed to have abandoned him. The idea of facing his end with some courage, even if it meant defying the town bullies, gave him a sense of purpose, a ray of light in the midst of darkness.

However, while his mind grappled with despair and the impulse to confront danger, Death remained a specter looming over his existence. Deep in his heart, his encounters with Death still resonated. She had become an unusual companion, a presence that observed and challenged him in critical moments.

Thus, amidst his confinement and torment, Cirilo found himself at a crossroads, weighing the value of his emotions, his desire to end his suffering, and the strange companionship of Death. Darkness and light, struggle and surrender, intertwined in his mind and heart, creating an internal conflict that would define the next step on his path towards redemption or resignation.

The town of Agua Fría awoke, the first lights of day timidly dispelling the darkness of the night. Cirilo, driven by his ambivalent determination, ventured through the alleyways. His gaze, weary but resolute, explored every corner in search of the troublemakers whose wrath he sought to attract.

The streets were quiet and tranquil, as if the town knew that something unusual was brewing in Cirilo's tormented heart. The market, once a bustling hub of life and activity, stretched out almost silently before him. As he advanced through the streets, his gaze caught the funeral procession that moved solemnly down the main street of the town. Sadness hung in the air, wrapped in tears and lamentations.

There, in front of the procession, Cirilo spotted José Torres, the father of the young woman who had chosen to end her life. José's figure radiated a pain that seemed to transcend the human, as if his heart had become an abyss of suffering. The weight of the loss was reflected in his reddened eyes and hunched back, carrying a pain no parent should bear. Beside the coffin walked Beda, the town's troubadour and the girl's guitar teacher, carrying his instrument on his back to bid farewell to the girl with the magic of his guitar.

Compassion and empathy overcame Cirilo at that moment. Despite his own torment, he saw himself mirrored in José's anguish. The story of the young girl who had lost hope resonated within him, and the reality that Death wasn't always a choice weighed on his soul. The irony of his self-destructive mission became evident. He had sought to confront Death in the most challenging way, but Death had already claimed its toll in ways he had not considered.

Amidst this moment of reflection, Death seemed like a distant yet watchful presence. Although he couldn't see her, he felt her influence in the scene, as if she were a silent echo of the destiny everyone would face at some point; the breeze that none can see, but that all feel.

Thus, Cirilo found himself at a turning point. The dark purpose that had led him to seek the town bullies was beginning to lose strength, replaced by a deeper understanding of life's fragility and how Death touched each of them in unexpected ways.

The day advanced with tense quietness in Agua Fría. The funeral procession had left a mark of melancholy in the air, and daily life seemed to move cautiously, as if the universe itself had become aware that something unusual was afoot.

Cirilo, in the grip of a fervor, traced every corner of the town. His eyes scoured every alley in search of his dark destiny. Death seemed to follow him like a silent shadow, always just out of reach.

And then, as a paradox in the midst of the emotionally charged air, the wife of the leader of the town bullies appeared. With elegance and haughtiness, she walked down the main street, accompanied by two servants struggling under the weight of shopping bags. The opportunity presented itself before him, tempting him with an easy way out, a way to close the circle he had opened himself.

Cirilo did not hesitate: he scooped up clumps of mud from the ground, and his arm rose in a daring arc. The mud found its target with miraculous precision, striking the woman's face, her clothing, and hair, leaving her figure, usually impeccable, stained and humiliated.

Amazement gripped the market. Townsfolk, who had watched the scene as if frozen in time, now burst into a chorus of murmurs and exclamations. No one could believe what their eyes were seeing. Cirilo's recklessness, his direct challenge to the troublemakers, had been an act of courage and madness at the same time.

The mud-streaked woman stood there, paralyzed by surprise and indignation. The servants dropped the shopping bags, also shocked by what they had witnessed. The air vibrated with change, as if a new story were being written at that very moment.

Cirilo, aware of the magnitude of his action, wasted no time. He mounted Donkey-xote and sped away. His escape, like a comet in the night, left a trail of uncertainty and admiration. Agua Fría would never be the same.

The next day, from the window of his house, Cirilo watched Death approach slowly. The atmosphere in the room seemed to throb to the beat of his heart. Every second passed like a resonant echo, like a melody fading into the distance. The wait was agonizing, as if the entire universe were turning its attention to his ramshackle home.

From the window, the scene unfolded like a tale from ancient times. Death, dressed as a black charro, advanced with a cadence

35

that seemed otherworldly, her steps resonating like echoes of eternity. By her side, two mexican hairless dogs with red eyes, guardians of the other side, followed her steps with a fixed and penetrating gaze.

Cirilo felt trapped in a trance between worlds, a state of awe and resignation. It had been he who had challenged Death, who had sought this encounter through bold yet desperate acts. Now, the moment he had longed for and feared was here, imminent and real. He was awestruck, thinking, 'My God, invoking Death is not the same as seeing her approach!'

He hurriedly made his way to Donkey-xote. He filled the water trough, released the muzzle, and set him free. He embraced and kissed him, dedicating some final words: 'I'm so sorry, Donkey-xote. I'm going ahead; I'll wait for you up there in heaven. You're free to go wherever you want; I no longer need you.'

He returned to his house, settled into his bed, ready to depart. Minutes stretched out like golden threads of a clock suspended in time. In his mind, memories paraded by, like images floating on a river of thoughts. Donkey-xote, his loyal companion, moved freely across the terrain, a distant echo of affection and farewell. Cirilo knew that, somewhere in the vast cosmos, their paths would cross again.

The moment arrived. Death drew near, her presence filling the room with an aura of solemnity. The hooves of her horse sounded like drums from another world, marking the rhythm of the end and the beginning. The dogs barked, voices from the threshold between life and death.

Cirilo lay down on his bed, closing his eyes as one closes the last pages of a worn but beloved book. The certainty of the end, the acceptance of destiny, blended in his mind with the echo of his words, a plea and a whisper to the infinite. Death advanced, reality and fantasy entwined in a mysterious embrace.

Shadows lengthened in the room, like hands reaching out to embrace him. Time paused for a moment, like a cosmic intermission. And in that moment of stillness and resignation, when the final sigh seemed imminent, something unexpected happened. A gentle ray of sunlight streamed through the window, painting the room with a golden glow.

Through the rotten gaps in the wooden walls of the house, he saw Death approach. He heard the hooves of her horse getting closer. The dogs continued to bark, as if announcing her arrival.

'This time she will take me!' exclaimed Cirilo.

The moment stretched out like a sad melody lingering in the wind. Death, in her black charro attire, moved with determination toward Cirilo's house. Each petal of each flower in the garden seemed to hold a silent plea, a final defense of life against the inescapable fate.

Death stopped in front of the wall of flowers, a palette of colors and shapes that seemed to dance in the wind. Her vacant eyes stared fixedly at the flowers, as if she could read in their petals the story of each day they had bloomed. The choice lay before her: brutality or respect, destruction or consideration. The flowers released their beautiful fragrance, begging for forgiveness. Death forgave most of them, but not all. Each flower that met its end beneath Death's blade left a trail of color on the wooden floor, a trace of beauty in the wake of an inexorable journey.

As Death advanced, Cirilo watched from the open window of his room. Finally, she reached the end of the path and stood among the fallen flowers. Through the open window, and, for a moment, her vacant eyes met Cirilo's. At that precise moment, something shifted in the air, as if time itself had paused to watch them. Death continued to advance, her steps resonating with the solemnity of a final judgment, until finally, she halted at Cirilo's door. Her empty eyes seemed to penetrate the man's soul, scrutinizing his thoughts, memories, and deepest desires.

Cirilo struggled to contain the thoughts that clamored to escape, but it was useless. In an instant, his restraint failed, and memories flooded his mind with the force of a torrent. Without warning, he was transported back to that fateful day when crossfire between two rival cartels tore his family away from his side. The faces of his wife and children appeared in his mind— their smiles, their voices, the weight of them in his arms. But he also saw the horror, the panic, and the pain in their eyes as violence erupted around them. Blood spilled on the ground, cries of pain, and helplessness merged into a memory he could never erase.

Death observed every fragment of that memory, every emotion that accompanied it. She could feel Cirilo's heart breaking in that moment, the weight of guilt and remorse crushing him like a stone. She saw his tears, his desperation, his plea for an end that never came.

Still the memories battered Cirilo. He embraced the graves of his family, prayed with a shattered heart, cried tears that seemed endless. Death, a silent witness to this suffering, could feel the survivor's anguish, the man's dilemma of yearning to join those he had lost but also fearing to leave.

Amidst that whirlwind of thoughts and emotions, Death remained undisturbed. She wasn't indifferent to human pain, but her role was inexorable, a path all must tread.

Death unraveled the threads of Cirilo's family history, weaving a tapestry of tragedy and sorrow that spanned generations. Each narrative, each tragic event, seemed a key piece in a puzzle of shared suffering. As she delved into ancestral memories, Death watched how the cycle of loss and lamentation repeated itself, like a painful echo reverberating through time.

Cirilo's grandfather, Don Anastasio Flores, had been another link in this chain of suffering. The chaos and violence of the Mexican Revolution of 1910 had torn his family apart. The taking of Zacatecas, a showdown that marked a turning point for the revolution, left a deep scar on Don Anastasio's life. Just like Cirilo, he had lost his family, caught in the crossfire between federal soldiers and Pancho Villa's Northern Division. The insurgents won the battle, but his grandfather lost everything.

Death contemplated the sadness in Don Anastasio's eyes, the heavy burden of having survived when those he loved had been taken. The life that followed was nothing but a constant echo of loss. Poverty, illness, and pain became unavoidable companions as Don Anastasio struggled for justice and confronted the powerful who had caused so much suffering. Yet his struggle only fueled the flames of repression and, in the end, cost him his life, a fate not so different from Cirilo's.

Death, impassive, perceived the unbreakable chain that bound Cirilo to his grandfather, and to many more souls who had shared similar destinies. Amidst this mosaic of loss, Death also saw the courage and resilience that had characterized these souls, their desire to confront adversity, even if the outcome seemed inevitable.

Death continued her journey through memories, delving into the deepest roots of the Flores family's history. In the early days of the struggle for Mexican Independence in 1810, the figure of Don Hermenegildo Flores emerged as a symbol of love, loss, and resistance.

In the days when the flame of Independence burned brightly, Don Hermenegildo lived passionately with his beloved family in Guanajuato. His home was filled with laughter, affection, and hope for a future free from colonial oppression. But fate took a cruel turn when war loomed over the Alhóndiga de Granaditas. Death snatched away his dearest loved ones in a bloodbath that would seal his destiny irrevocably. Death witnessed how Don Hermenegildo clung to hope even as his world crumbled. His courage led him to raise his voice in search of justice, to challenge the oppressors, and to fight for what he believed was right. However, his challenge was met with furious retaliation from the powerful, and once again history repeated itself: Don Hermenegildo's life extinguished was by those he had defied.

Death saw in these intertwined threads of suffering and resistance a story that repeated itself across generations. Each of the Flores men, from the great-grandfather to Cirilo, had lost their loved ones, and each had raised their voice against injustice and faced the consequences. It was a narrative that transcended time, woven with threads of sadness and courage, a tapestry of lives interconnected by suffering and struggle, of humanity's capacity to confront adversity with bravery and hope.

The scene transformed into a manifestation of nature itself, an encounter between the human realm and the animal kingdom, between the earthly and the divine. At that moment, something magical and beautiful began: hundreds of monarch butterflies landed on the four crosses on the far side of the house, completely covering them. In their delicate fragility and radiance, they wove a veil of wonder that guarded the Flores' story. Each wing, a fragment of history; each flutter, a heartbeat of that lineage pierced by struggle and loss.

Death, who had been about to claim Cirilo, remained motionless before the spectacle. That corner of Agua Fría was filled with a strange vibration, a connection between worlds that seemed to defy even Death herself. But as the butterflies wove their dance of life and beauty, the dogs, guardians of the tangible and the mundane, fought to protect their claimed space from intrusion, and attempted to scare away the delicate creatures. They barked and howled in the face of what they couldn't comprehend.

Then, from above, a celestial light descended, like a ray of knowledge and truth, illuminating every corner of the land. That light, a divine decree, resonated in the hearts of all. It was a call to break the painful cycles, to end the recurrences of tragedies that had marked Mexico's history. A message of hope and transformation.

Death, witnessing this act of communion between the human, the animal, and the divine, felt a profound reverence for the grandeur of life and its intricate interconnection. The scythe she had held firmly became a symbol of renewal rather than a tool of inexorable destiny. She became aware that her role was not only to take souls but also to bear witness to the human capacity to change, to heal, and to create a different future.

Death, in her determination to change Cirilo's fate, had taken radical steps to eliminate anything that could threaten his new life. The garden, once filled with flowers, was now marked by the violence of the scythe, as if time itself had been interrupted and rewritten. ~~Donkey-ote,~~ Donkey-xote, Cirilo's loyal companion, had been ripped from his life, and the crows, those ill omens, lay dead on the ground. The town troublemakers had also fallen, and Death had removed everything that was not good for Cirilo.

However, Death had not fully understood the complexity of human emotions. While trying to clear Cirilo's path, she couldn't erase the memories, the love, and the bonds that had been woven over so many years. The donkey's death was another wound, a painful reminder of the fragility of existence and the deep connections forged in life.

Cirilo, alone with his grief, now faced a new chapter in his life, one where the cycle of violence had been broken but where those who had been part of his world had also been taken away. In his bed, he wept for the loss of his loyal friend, just as he had cried for his wife, his children, and his ancestors. Sobs wracked his body. He was ready to depart from that life, but once again he had failed. He turned around in his bed to weep in silence. Amid his depression, he lamented: 'Farewell, Donkey-xote, faithful friend! You've found the peace that I cannot reach. Who will bury Donkey-xote? I don't have the strength to do it.'

Death, who had tried to alter Cirilo's course with a noble gesture, realized that she couldn't completely eliminate human suffering. Life and death were part of the same cycle and couldn't be separated so easily. Cirilo's tears echoed the sadness that had permeated throughout generations of his family.

The sky darkened, and the gathering storm seemed to be the physical reflection of the tempest stirring within Cirilo. The thunderous roar of lightning resonated in his mind, as if each thunderclap were an echo of his own internal torment. Rain pounded on the roof of his house with fury, as if the sky itself were weeping on his behalf.

Cirilo lay in his bed, assailed by visions. The faces of his loved ones lost throughout the generations seemed to gaze at him from the shadows, filling his dreams with overwhelming melancholy. The void in his heart threatened to swallow him whole.

Amid his fever, Cirilo could still feel the closeness of Death. But now, the visions were crueler, more disturbing. In his delirium, Death paraded him through the streets of Agua Fría, bound and tied, exhibiting him as a trophy before the entire town. It was as if Death were exploring the darkest corners of his psyche, unearthing his deepest fears and exposing them to the world.

The night passed in a whirlwind of ragged visions as the storm raged outside and the fever ate away at his body. Darkness embraced him tightly, enveloping him in a cloak of despair. But still, there was a trace of resistance in Cirilo's soul. A spark of will to fight against the suffering that had plagued him for so long.

The loneliest night of his existence was coming to an end, giving way to dawn. The sky began to lighten, and the storm gradually subsided. Cirilo, exhausted and soaked in sweat, opened his eyes slowly. Although the storm in his mind had not completely dissipated, there was a new determination in his gaze. The struggle to find meaning in his life, to overcome the weight of his family's history, and to confront Death on his own terms was far from over. And amid the darkness and adversity, he clung to the hope that someday he might find the redemption and peace he so deeply longed for.

The sun streamed in through the gaps in the rotted walls, marking the beginning of a beautiful day, and Cirilo could hear footsteps approaching. Cirilo dragged himself to the front door. Mr. Smith smiled in greeting. An American lawyer representing the farmers exposed to chemicals in California, Mr. Smith had been litigating against the big pesticide companies for over fifteen years, companies with millions of dollars to defend themselves against a lawyer with little renown and few resources. Yet, he was the only one willing to represent the farmers in a seemingly hopeless cause.

The lawyer pushed open the wooden door. With a big smile, he spoke to him in his bright American accent: 'Wake up, Cirilo! Today is a good day to celebrate. We won your case in court. You can retire comfortably.'

Mr. Smith opened a briefcase filled with American dollars. Cirilo picked up a stack of hundred-dollar bills and, smelling it, said: 'Manure! You come to me when I no longer need you!'

'Relax, Cirilo. You're getting bitter too soon. Take a minute. With this, you can travel all over Mexico. Enjoy your money,' Mr. Smith suggested.

Cirilo looked at the bills with a mixture of disbelief and detachment. For years, he had dreamed of relief from his hardships, of an opportunity to leave behind the cycle of suffering that had marked his life. And now, at a moment when those dreams seemed within his grasp, he found himself in such a despondent mood that not even the promise of wealth could coax a smile from him.

Mr. Smith's words echoed in his head, but Cirilo remained bound to his inner demons. The courtroom victory couldn't erase painful memories or heal the emotional wounds that had tormented him for so long. The money that had promised liberation, now that it was here, had become only another burden on his conscience.

'You don't understand, Mr. Smith. It's no longer just about money. I've carried my family's sorrows for generations. Suffering is rooted in my history and my being. I can't simply rid myself of it with bills,' Cirilo replied with a subdued voice.

The lawyer looked at him with compassion and sat down beside him. He had fought alongside Cirilo in court, had heard his story, and knew the depth of his suffering. He understood that money couldn't erase the past, but he also believed in people's capacity to find a new way of life, even after the most challenging adversities.

'I understand that the pain you've carried is overwhelming, Cirilo. But this victory gives you the opportunity to do something new, to change your path and find renewed meaning in life. Money can open doors that were once closed and give you the freedom to explore whatever you wish,' Mr. Smith said sincerely.

Cirilo regarded the lawyer with a doubtful look. He knew that Mr. Smith was partly right, but he also felt trapped in his own mindset and ingrained thought patterns.

The room fell into a tense silence, broken only by the whisper of the wind coming through the window. Cirilo contemplated the bills in his hands, tangible symbols of an opportunity that seemed distant to him. The lawyer, patient and understanding, waited for Cirilo to find his way through the fog of his emotions.

Finally, after a long moment of reflection, Cirilo sighed deeply and looked at Mr. Smith with a mixture of determination and hope in his eyes. It was the beginning of a new chapter in his life, a chapter in which he would have to confront his inner demons and find his own redemption. 'Perhaps you're right, Mr. Smith. Maybe it's time to seek a new purpose in my life and leave the weight of the past behind. But it won't be easy,' Cirilo said with a firm voice.

The lawyer nodded with a warm smile and stood up. 'No one said it would be easy, Cirilo. But I'm confident that you have the strength to face whatever comes. I'll support you in whatever you need,' Mr. Smith affirmed.

Cirilo looked at the bills in his hands once more and then raised his gaze to the future, with a mixture of nervousness and determination. The opportunity to start anew was there, and he alone could determine how he would write the next chapter of his story.

Following the lawyer's advice, Cirilo set off to travel throughout Mexico. The conversion of dollars to Mexican pesos allowed him to eat well and dress better. The dentist provided him with a new set of teeth, and for the first time, Cirilo no longer felt arthritis pain thanks to the medical treatment he could now afford.

Although his nervous tic still persisted, it was more manageable with medical care. He helped all those who had ever extended a helping hand to him and paid off each of his debts. He provided support to the homeless, the abandoned, the forgotten, to people with disabilities, the terminally ill, orphans, and widows. Additionally, he granted loans to small business owners who, over time, boosted the economy of Agua Fría and thrived for many years, generating wealth for future generations.

For many years, Cirilo traveled across Mexico and explored every corner of the country. One day, while in the state of Veracruz, he entered a restaurant and ordered a dish of huatape de acamayas. Upon tasting it, tears rolled down his cheeks as he remembered his childhood. In the rivers of Agua Fría, there were almost no acamayas left; they were practically extinct and could only be found in hatcheries. That day, Cirilo enjoyed three plates of huatape de acamayas.

Finally, exhausted from his travels, he decided to return to Agua Fría. There, he discovered an old hacienda transformed into the Agua Fría Hotel.

He patiently waited every day, sitting on the hotel's terrace, until one morning he spotted a familiar silhouette atop Cerro de la Cruz. Cirilo burst into laughter. There she was again, dressed in her black charro outfit, riding her jet-black horse.

He stood up and walked towards her.

'I can't deny it, Death, I owe you my life,' Cirilo said, static and joyful. 'You saved me! I was saved by Death! And if it's not too much trouble, Death, in my next life, I wish to be Mexican again.'

Laughing, he mounted the jet-black horse and rode with Death until both disappeared over the horizon behind Cerro de la Cruz, and Cirilo Flores was never heard from again.

Cirilo became a legend in Agua Fría. His story of transformation, resilience, and redemption was shared from generation to generation. People found inspiration in his example and drew strength in difficult times by remembering how Cirilo had faced his own darkness and found light.

The Agua Fría Hotel, in the old hacienda, became a place of pilgrimage for those seeking hope and renewal. The gardens bloomed with the same flowers Cirilo had admired in life, and the terrace from which he used to watch Cerro de la Cruz remained a sanctuary of peace.

The elders of Agua Fría shared stories of how Cirilo had touched their lives with his generosity and compassion. Children listened in awe as they imagined the adventures of this brave man who had defied Death and found a new beginning amid adversity.

Rumors that Cirilo was still alive somewhere in the country spread from mouth to mouth. It was said that sometimes, in moments of darkness, a silhouette on a jet-black horse appeared on the peak of Cerro de la Cruz, watching with understanding and love in their eyes.

People continued to find inspiration in Cirilo's story, remembering that life was full of challenges but also opportunities to transform suffering into growth and pain into hope. And so, Cirilo Flores, the man who had defied Death and found redemption, lived on in the memory and hearts of all those touched by his story.

Author's Note

In the intricate fabric of *The Law of the Mexican*, allegory blooms like a garden of intertwined meanings. Each character, each scene is a thread outlining crucial moments in Mexican history and its possible evolution. Through this intricate tapestry, the author aims to reflect Mexico's past and its constant quest to transcend its history.

Symbolism is the binding force holding together every detail of this narrative. Cirilo Flores emerges as an incarnation of the nation itself, carrying the weight of its history and the obstacles that have hindered its development. Donkey-xote, with its twisted name, stands as a symbol of the ignorance that has halted Mexico at every historical crossroads. The crows plundering the cornfield, in their destructive voracity, become the personification of the corruption that has plagued the country in every era. The town bullies, bearers of violence and chaos, give voice to the dark moments that have shadowed Mexico's path.

Death, in its unusual role, adopts an intriguing duality. Her decision not to take Cirilo but to strip him of the burdens that bound him to the ground transcends the somber image we often associate with her. Here, Death is an agent of transformation, a catalyst for the regeneration of a Mexico burdened by the shadows of its history.

The three historical recurrences unfold like the stages of a rite of passage, where Mexico faces challenging tests and then rises with a renewed sense of purpose. The first, during the War of Independence in 1810, symbolizes the beginning of the struggle for freedom and self-determination. The second, the Mexican Revolution in 1910, emerged as an era of turmoil and change, marking the fight for social justice and equality.

Finally, in 2010, amid conflicts stemming from drug cartels, hope looms on the horizon. Mexico breaks free from the chains that tied it to its recurring history of violence and spreads its wings toward the possibility of a new era. Here, the author's message is clear: historical recurrences are not an immutable destiny but a call to action and change.

Ultimately, *The Law of the Mexican* becomes a powerful reflection of Mexico's resilience and capacity for transformation. Through the masterful use of symbols and metaphors, the author conveys a promise of progress and prosperity. In these pages, Mexico's history and future intertwine in a hopeful dance that invites the reader to imagine a brighter tomorrow and embark on a journey of redemption and transcendence.

Welcome to the future!

The Doors

The greatest disillusionment someone can face in life is seeing the person they love the most fall from grace. This is what happened to Felipa when she found her mother with a lover. A few days later, her mother abandoned the entire family to be with that man, and from then on, misfortunes never stopped pouring over their home.

Even though three years had passed since the abandonment, every time the memory of that experience came to Felipa's mind, she felt hatred and resentment, just as she did at this very moment.

The doors of memory swung open relentlessly, letting out the memories Felipa had tried to bury deep in her heart. Every time she closed her eyes, she could feel the echo of betrayal and agony that had haunted her since that fateful day. Despite her efforts to move forward, the emotional scars remain fresh, as if time had frozen in that moment of despair.

Felipa was in the small garden of the house where she had grown up. The scent of the flowers, which used to bring her comfort, now only seemed to fan the sadness inside her. While the sun smiled on the horizon, a shadow loomed over her, reminding her that her mother had chosen to abandon her family in pursuit of a romantic passion.

The wind whispered stories of loneliness and loss as leaves gently fell to the ground. Felipa clutched an old diary she had kept hidden in her room for years. Every page was filled with letters that expressed her pain and confusion. The diary was a way to release emotions she found impossible to speak aloud, but most importantly, it was also where she had written over thirty songs that she had composed herself. Flipping through the yellowed pages, she came across an entry that made her pause. It was a letter her mother had written to her shortly before leaving. The words were a whirlwind of apologies and explanations, but also of love and hope. Felipa couldn't help but shed tears as she read the lines written by the same hand that had held her as a child.

Her mother's words echoed in her mind: 'Sometimes, love takes us down painful and complicated paths. But never doubt that, despite my mistakes, I have always loved you and will always love you.'

It was time for dinner, and the tempting aroma of homemade food wafted through every corner of the house. The sun, weary after a long day, cast golden rays that seemed to caress the brightly painted walls. Nana María, with her silver hair and soft, wise voice, called Felipa to the table with a kind gesture.

As they gathered around the table, sunlight streamed through the windows, creating a play of light and shadow in the room. Her plate was filled with regional delicacies, each bite a tribute to the roots and culture of Agua Fría. Nana María, with her colorful apron and skilled hands, served with love and dedication.

While Felipa savored the first bite, Nana María began to speak with a calm yet meaningful voice.

'Mexico is magical, but also wild,' she whispered, as if her words carried the echo of centuries of history and legends that had shaped the country. She looked at Felipa with her eyes full of experience, as if through her gaze, she could convey the very essence of the land she loved. 'And that's how the world sees us, thanks to the news,' she continued, sighing deeply. There was a trace of sadness in her words, as if she were battling the distorted perceptions that often prevailed in the media. 'Mexico is a paradise on earth, but we Mexicans ruin everything,' she added with a hint of self-criticism.

While Felipa stared at the plate of chicken with vegetables, her mind drifted. Raindrops gently tapped against the window, creating a monotonous rhythm that seemed to accompany her thoughts. The comforting aroma of homemade food couldn't penetrate the shell of melancholy that enveloped her heart. It had been a terrible, dull day for her, a succession of hours that dragged on as if time itself had stopped. She felt exhausted from the night before, as if she had been fighting an invisible battle while the world slept, oblivious to her torment.

Nothing improved her mood. Not even the murmur of the radio in the corner of the kitchen, with its cheerful voices and songs that used to make her smile. It was as if a heavy shadow loomed over her spirit, darkening any glimmer of joy that tried to emerge.

She simply wished to disappear. To close her eyes and fade into the mist of her thoughts, away from the reality that tormented her. She longed for a refuge where she could leave behind the worries and expectations that weighed on her young shoulders. But where would she find that refuge? How could she escape the spiral of emotions that trapped her?

In the distance, the sky was tinged with golden and rosy hues as the sun prepared to bid farewell to the day. Felipa felt a strange mix of hopelessness and resignation. Although the weight of her situation wouldn't disappear overnight, the beauty of the sunset reminded her that life could also be beautiful, that tough moments would eventually give way to new dawns and opportunities.

With a deep sigh, Felipa averted her gaze from her plate. The house, with its familiar corners, took on a different hue under the soft light of the sunset. The shadows seemed gentler, less menacing. Perhaps, she thought, there was a way through the darkness, a way to transform her struggle into strength.

Without saying a word to Nana María, Felipa rose from the table. She retreated to her room like a butterfly seeking refuge in a quiet corner of the garden. The weight of the day was reflected in her gaze, a gaze that had seen more than her young years should have witnessed.

As she passed through the living room, Felipa's senses were enveloped in a mist of sweet melancholy. An intense scent of marigold flowers danced in the air, carrying with it echoes of ancient traditions. She closed her eyes, allowing herself for a moment to slip into the nostalgia that emanated from the environment. The fragrance transported her to simpler times, to days of shared laughter and warm embraces.

Opening her eyes, her gaze found the altar of the Day of the Dead that Nana María had erected with devotion. The altar, like a sanctuary in the middle of the room, was adorned with yellow flowers that seemed to light up like little flames of hope amidst the darkness. The petals intertwined in a vibrant embrace, as if each flower had a story to tell.

The food laid out on the altar was a tribute to the departed, an invitation for them to join in the feast of memories and affection. Each bite was meant to bring back loved ones for a moment, a fleeting reconciliation between the world of the living and the departed.

Photographs of family members who had crossed the threshold into eternity were arranged with careful tenderness. Each face was a link to the past, a way to keep alive the connection with those who had left a mark on Felipa's life. Her grandfather's eyes seemed to find hers, a gaze that transcended time and space.

Felipa felt a sense of calm and reverence as she gazed at the altar. The flames of the candles danced serenely, filling the room with a soft glow. As the night advanced, the shadows cast by the candlelight seemed to weave a story of their own on the walls, a wordless narration that spoke of love and loss, of presence and absence.

Felipa allowed herself to connect with the memories and feelings that had shaped her journey. She knew that, even though loved ones were no longer physically present, their influence endured in every beat of her heart. The Day of the Dead altar was more than a ritual display; it was a bridge to understanding that, like the flame and the shadow, life and death are intertwined in an eternal dance of transformation.

Then, as she always did, Felipa turned to the photo of her sister Celeste. The snapshot, framed with a delicacy that seemed to capture eternity in a small rectangle, was carefully placed on the altar. It was as if the very paper resonated with the essence of the young woman who was no longer there, who had left a trail of joy in her wake.

The memory of that beach day in Tecolutla, a day that time could never erase, emerged in Felipa's mind like the caress of the sea breeze. The waves roared in a rhythmic ballet with the breeze, and the sun painted golden glimmers on the water. Celeste's classmates laughed and played, their voices filling the air with the melody of youth. It was a day that seemed sewn with golden threads in the fabric of memory, a day that had captured two sisters in its warm embrace.

It had been a lucky day for Felipa, a day when her sister's invitation to join the beach adventure opened a door to shared moments that had never been so vibrant, so full of life. They had never been happier together then in those moments, never imagining that misfortune, always lurking in the shadows, would strike them with overwhelming cruelty right then. Destiny, inscrutable and often relentless, had taken from them what they loved most in the world.

They discovered, in a cruel and painful way, that happiness was fleeting, a gift that could be torn from their hands in an instant. In Felipa's mind, the image of that radiant day at the beach intertwined with the memory of the pain that followed, like a bittersweet counterpoint in life's symphony.

Felipa pulled her gaze from the altar and went on through the deepening darkness of the house. As she walked through the familiar hallways, Felipa spoke with her sister in whispers of thought, as if her words could transcend the boundaries of life and death. 'Who would have imagined, sister, that the photo from Tecolutla would be the same one they'd use above your obituary?' Her inner voice trembled with the echo of unspoken words. 'At least, in that picture, you looked beautiful, with your best smile,' she murmured tenderly. It was as if her words were a silent offering to her sister's memory, an attempt to convey the beauty of her spirit through the shadows of the past.

Entering her room, a wave of pain swept over her like the wind that shakes down leaves in autumn. The room, a treasure chest of shared memories and the hopes of a future that would never materialize, seemed to come to life with its silent sighs and whispering shadows. The light filtering through the curtains seemed to have a melancholic tone, as if the sun itself shared the weight of the sadness reflected in Felipa's eyes.

The air, heavy with intertwined memories, resonated with echoes of the past. And in that intimate space, where the walls seemed to be mute witnesses to the history of a broken family, Felipa felt a cold hand brushing her heart. The image of her sister appeared before her eyes with a shocking clarity, as if every object in the room vibrated in unison with the pain that dwelled within her.

A shiver, like a discordant note in the symphony of life, coursed through Felipa's body. Twisted and heart-wrenching images of the past emerged like fragments of an unforgettable dream. The sea, once a symbol of freedom and shared joy with her sister, was now a dark abyss that threatened to engulf her.

The memory of the moment they retrieved her sister's lifeless body from the sea was etched into Felipa's memory like a tattoo on the soul. The sound of the waves seemed to transform into a chorus of lamentations, and the wind whispered tragic tales as tears mixed with salt water. It was a wound that would never fully heal, a knot in the heart that tightened with every beat.

Since that fateful moment, Felipa had developed an intense fear of water. Even the sound of rain hitting the windows reminded her of the fragility of life and the relentless hunger of death.

In the dark room, Felipa sank onto her bed, feeling the weight of the past like an anchor threatening to drag her into the depths. Tears slipped down her cheeks as the room's silence filled with the echo of her pain.

Yet as she lay there in the dark, laden with emotions and memories, Felipa found a glimmer of solace in the idea that, although water frightened her and life had taken her sister down an unfathomable path, their love remained a bridge between worlds. She allowed herself to believe that somehow the bond between them would transcend distance and time, keeping a connection alive that not even death could break.

The pain receded for a moment and Felipa lifted her head from the blankets, as a more mundane fear reasserted itself. She also suffered from arachnophobia, a terror that lurked in the corners of her mind like a dark shadow that would not fade. Every day, when she returned from school, the ritual of inspecting her room became a dance of caution, as if she were searching for invisible traces of creatures that had tormented her since the day a classmate unleashed the chaos of her fear.

The room, which had once been her refuge of dreams and serene thoughts, now felt like a minefield. The bed, every corner, even the shadows on the wall, everything needed to be thoroughly inspected before she could sleep.

It all began when a schoolmate came to class with four tarantulas hanging from his chest. The boy, with a sinister smile and an air of triumph, walked through the school corridors like a champion of the grotesque. With twisted pride he displayed the spiders, each one the size of a human fist.

The other boys watched with a mixture of fascination and repulsion as the spiders crawled in his hands, their spiky legs touching the air in a choreography of horrors. The girls screamed and looked away, but Felipa was paralyzed by the macabre spectacle unfolding before her eyes. The images of the tarantulas, with their menacing bodies and spiky legs, were etched into her mind.

From that moment on, her relationship with spiders turned into a constant battle between the desire to overcome her fear and the anguish that gripped her mind. Spiders, once just harmless insects, had become a symbol of an unquenchable fear.

Felipa's skin prickled at the mere thought of the texture of their bodies.

When she tried to rationalize her fear, the images of the tarantulas hanging from the boy's chest resurfaced in her mind, like ghosts that could not be banished. It was as if her memory had been hijacked by the event, and the present remained a constant struggle between the desire to overcome her fear and the paralyzing force of the phobia.

The boys used to venture to a place known in their small universe as 'the door,' a threshold to the unknown that was embedded in their imagination and in the geography of the place. There, in that remote place beyond the limits of the town, a mysterious rocky outcrop rose like a natural monument, a place where tarantulas, guardians of arcane secrets, had made their home. The stories that circulated in their youthful whispers spoke of hidden nests under the stone lid, a swarm of arachnids waiting to be discovered by daring hands.

What would be a perilous and frightening endeavor for some had become a rite of passage for these audacious boys, a challenge to nature itself. With courage mixed with the recklessness of youth, they dared to turn over any stone, each one holding the possibility of an unexpected encounter with the dark world of tarantulas. A V-shaped stick, like a magic wand summoning the hairy creatures, was their tool to extract them from their hiding places.

With skilled hands and a confidence bordering on audacity, they pulled the tarantulas from their nests, gripping them with the curve of the stick, as if they were trophies from a forbidden world. The dance of spider and stick, of skill and bravery, culminated in a surgical ritual. With meticulous determination, they turned the tarantula, as if they were revealing its vulnerable belly to the world. Nail clippers, a cutting blade transformed into a tool of dominion, swiftly extracted the lethal fangs.

Draining the venom, the liquid that held the deadly power of these creatures, transformed the tarantulas into defenseless beings, as if the essence of their danger had evaporated with each drop. The ritual, a mixture of dominion and transformation, left the spiders harmless, turning them into marionettes without strings in the hands of the boys.

But despite this artificial innocence, the terror persisted in the memories of those who had witnessed it. The act of looking at these tarantulas, now disarmed, surpassed any fear of their deadly power. They were like ghosts of their former selves; though stripped of their earthly power, their presence still held all the terror of the first encounter.

However, Felipa remained in the shadow of understanding. The reckless exploits of these daring boys were an enigma to her, an inexplicable paradox. While these boys ventured into the world with fearless confidence, she was trapped in the web of her own fears, unable to comprehend how they could face the unknown as easily as breathing.

From the vantage point of her fear, Felipa wondered how the boys seemed to ignore terror, while she struggled in the clutches of apprehension. Each new day presented itself as a challenge, a door that opened into the unknown, an opportunity to confront her own fears and discover the latent power within herself. But, like the disarmed tarantulas, her courage had become fragile, and facing the dawn seemed like an odyssey that required a bravery she had not yet discovered.

Yet night brought her no relief. The arrival of darkness was agony for Felipa; the dark opened into an entanglement of uncertainty in which she was lost without a compass or guide.

The stars, points of flickering light on the black canvas of the sky, offered her no solace. Every night, as she closed her eyes, she entered a realm of nightmares, a stage where the rules were dictated by forces beyond her control.

She shifted on her bed. Shadows lengthened. She wished the night could be delayed, that the sun would retain its last breath of radiance. However, the inevitability of the cycle continued its course, and the day faded with the same certainty as the shadows conquered the terrain.

Felipa knew she had to succumb to the call of sleep. But resistance persisted in her spirit like a flame. The room, that sanctuary of dreams and shadows, was steeped in dense energies, as if the weight of her own fear had permeated the very walls.

And then they appeared, like lurking shadows creeping from the depths of the darkness. Four entities, each carrying a unique terror. The mirror, a distorted reflection of her own fears, confronted her with deformed versions of herself. The doors, guardians of invisible thresholds, were endless mazes that led nowhere. The water, a liquid mass that dragged her into the depths, immersed her in spiritual suffocation. And then, the prowler, the Nahual, an enigmatic creature that dwelled on the thin line between the human and the spiritual world, brought with it a promise of unfathomable darkness.

These entities, like puppets in a macabre theater, presented themselves in her dream world to torment her. Every night, destiny seemed to bring a new affliction, a nightmare that entered her mind and coiled like a venomous snake. The immobility of her sleep offered no escape; it was as if her will faded into the blackness of the night, leaving her at the mercy of these tormenting specters.

Felipa struggled, resisted, tried to stay awake for as long as possible, like a mariner on a drifting raft trying to avoid the whirlpools and raging currents. But despite her heroic efforts, drowsiness always overcame her, the abyss inexorably dragged her down, and her closed eyes unlocked the door to a world where her own terror was master and lord. Thus, the night became a battlefield in which Felipa faced the shadows of her fear. Every dawn, she emerged from the darkness as a tired but persistent warrior, ready to face another day.

That night, darkness brought with it the doors. Felipa found herself trapped in a tangle of a thousand thresholds, each laden with intricate symbolism. Each door, a portal to the unknown, carried the weight of her destiny, of her path through life. Some were like hidden treasures, opening onto blessings and successes, while others were portals to misfortune and adversity.

Each door, a microcosm of opportunity or disadvantage, stood as an enigma that could only be solved by those whose names were written in the stars. The doors, which seemed simple in their form, were the guardians of a complex labyrinth of choices and intertwined destinies.

Felipa, like an explorer in a forest of possibilities, found herself in the midst of this network of doors. However, she did not seek for herself those that opened to success or triumph. She, brave and noble in her longing, clung to the doors that were for others: the doors of blessings, of peace, of love, of wisdom. She gazed at them with hopeful eyes, as if she could reach them with the stretch of her hand.

The search was arduous and tenacious on that silent night. Each door, with its unique meaning and innate mystery, resisted being revealed. Felipa, in her tireless exploration, sought to discover which of these magical doors would open for her. Disappointment crept into her heart, like a dark shadow threatening to overshadow her hope. Among the doors, only one offered its path.

There were moments when temptation caressed her like a whisper in the wind. The only door that was willing to yield to her touch called to her, an invitation to cross into the unknown. But Felipa, with an inner strength that seemed to grow with every challenge, held herself back, resisting the ease of that choice. She knew that doors, like books, could not be judged by their outward appearances alone.

She persisted in her search, in her exploration of those dimensional passages. However, no matter how far she searched, the doors she longed for, those of blessings and prosperity, remained closed to her. In the vastness of that labyrinth, other people, their destinies woven in different cosmic fabrics, walked through those doors with ease. Doors of prosperity, of abundance, of knowledge, of life, of happiness. Their luck seemed like a gift from the gods, and envy grew in Felipa's heart like a poisonous plant.

The only door that offered itself, like a beacon in the darkness, patiently awaited her choice. But Felipa, aware of the importance of her decision, chose to continue her search. In the past, she had tried to cross that door on two occasions, but the result had been defeat. With wisdom born from failure, she preferred to wait, trusting that someday, in some corner of the labyrinth of her destiny, a more opportune door would appear before her tired eyes.

Dawn brought with it the feeling of having sailed through dark and treacherous seas during the night. Felipa, with her eyes that seemed like faint beacons in the mist, prepared herself to face a new school day, a battle against the fatigue that had besieged her like an insidious shadow. The lack of sleep had left its mark on her face, a canvas pale and marked by the traces of insomnia.

Every step she took seemed like a titanic effort, as if she were dragging invisible chains that threatened to pull her back into the darkness of the previous night. Her energy was depleted, her thoughts clouded by a fog that was both physical and emotional. She had faced the internal storms that ravaged her while the world was plunged into the silence of the night, and now she faced the expectations of the day with a will that seemed almost extinguished.

Nana María helped her get dressed. Her hands were warm and comforting, but there was an abyss between them, an abyss forged in the gap between what Felipa experienced in the darkness of her nightmares and what Nana María could understand. Felipa's efforts to explain her nighttime sufferings collided with the wall of disbelief, and her words, like leaves carried by the wind, seemed to vanish into the air.

Nana María, in her wisdom and maternal love, clung to an explanation that fit her understanding of the world: 'You have to stop watching horror movies, they're not good for you!' she said, as if the shadows that haunted Felipa could be dispelled by the simple logic of reality. But the demons that pursued her in her dreams were not the result of fictional movies but manifestations of her own fear and anxiety.

Nana María's indifference, though unintentional, echoed in Felipa's soul. The young girl was caught between the need to be understood and the harsh reality of a lack of understanding. Silent tears were her response to the disconnection between her words and the perceptions of others.

Always following on the heels of Nana María's well-intentioned misunderstandings, a mantra echoed: 'You are a very refined and fortunate young lady, with a bright future ahead!' The affirmation repeated itself every morning like an echo, a promise of a better tomorrow. However, the bright future seemed to be framed by the shadows of the night, and Felipa struggled to find the bridge that connected her nighttime anxieties to the bright path promised to her.

Thus, at the crossroads between incomprehension and the promise of hope, Felipa faced each day like a butterfly struggling to emerge from its chrysalis. Her tired eyes continued to gaze at the horizon, where the doors of destiny and the doors of her heart intertwined in a dance of possibilities and mysteries.

Every morning, after Nana María had delivered her kind, misguided encouragement, Felipa headed to school, like an actress playing a role in a drama where she didn't feel she belonged. In her classroom, she sat at her desk, but her mind wandered far away, in a world where dreams were her only company. Meanwhile, life passed around her like a dance she couldn't join. She felt like delicate glass, on the verge of shattering at the slightest touch. Lost in her own struggle, she longed for refuge, a place where her troubles could dissolve.

In the classroom, time passed at a slow and painful pace. Every lesson, every formula, seemed like an insurmountable mountain. Instead of being a sanctuary of learning, school became a maze of frustration and anxiety. Concentration slipped through her fingers like sand.

Amidst this internal struggle, school transformed into a battlefield where her own mind became the enemy. The simple act of sitting in the classroom became an act of resistance, a struggle to stay afloat in a sea of difficulties. Every step forward seemed to be followed by two steps back, as if the current of time were dragging her with a force beyond her control.

However, despite the storm that surrounded her, there was a glimmer of determination in Felipa's heart. She persisted in her search for meaning, for an escape, for a ray of light that could illuminate her path. Even as tears welled up in her eyes and frustration threatened to break her spirit, she moved forward, each day a test of her courage and perseverance. In her quest to find her place in the world, Felipa was woven with threads of hope, a narrative in constant evolution that would lead her through the doors to an uncertain but full-of-possibilities tomorrow.

That day, like so many others, the walk back home from school felt like crossing a bridge suspended between reality and the abyss of her thoughts. Every step, like a discordant note in an out-of-tune symphony, resonated in her ears and mingled with the incessant whispers inhabiting her mind. The outside world seemed like a blurry reflection of her own internal struggle, heavier with each passing day.

Dinner seemed like an insignificant distraction compared to the whirlwind raging within her. Bites barely touched her lips, as if her thoughts were the only diners at that banquet. Nana María couldn't help but express her worry. 'You're not eating enough, my child,' she said, while her gaze conveyed a sea of unspoken wishes.

However, food, which at another time might have been a source of comfort, had been relegated to the darkest corner of Felipa's priorities. The monsters that haunted her, creatures born of her fears and anxieties, had grown into giants that dominated her mind. Every night, as the moon rose in the sky, the monsters rose like enlarging shadows, threatening to devour her whole.

Felipa knew that she herself, in a cruel paradox, had contributed to nurturing these monsters. Every thought of fear, every doubt and anxiety, was like a drop in a river that grew in ferocity over time. She recognized her role in the torment that consumed her, as if she were an unwitting alchemist turning her emotions into indomitable monsters.

After dinner, she retreated to her sanctuary, her room, to complete her homework. Every problem solved, every formula mastered, was like a small triumph that reminded her she could still conquer her challenges. But it was music that allowed her to momentarily escape the clutches of her thoughts.

The guitar strings vibrated under her fingers, like whispers from another reality, from another world. Melodies flowed like rivers of emotions seeking an outlet. Each chord was a glimmer of light amidst the darkness that enveloped her.

Hours passed like leaves in the wind as Felipa played until her fingers ached and her thoughts began to yield ground. The guitar, like a lighthouse in the night, guided her through the turbulent waters of her mind. Music, like a magical key, unlocked the doors of her emotions and allowed tears and sighs to flow like a river. Each chord, each tremolo, was a statement of her resistance, of her determination to keep the flame of her spirit alive amidst the darkness. In the sanctuary of her room, among the notes that danced in the air, Felipa wrote her own song of struggle and hope, a melody that guided her through the night and toward a new dawn. Her tape recorder was her best friend, although worn by the years, it still managed to immortalize Felipa's songs.

When the tragic loss of Celeste cast its shadow over the family, Felipa clung to the acoustic guitar that had once belonged to her sister. The strings now resonated like an echo of shared memories, a tangible connection to the spirit of the one who had gone too soon. In her hands, the guitar became a bridge between the earthly world and the realm of memories.

Felipa discovered in the guitar strings a way to translate her pain into art. As the notes intertwined in the air, her heart found a voice in the songs she began to compose. Her room became a sanctuary where her spirit could flow freely, where thoughts and feelings that had been silenced found an outlet.

The first song that emerged from her heart and her guitar was titled 'Somewhere.' The words, like brushstrokes on a blank canvas, took shape on her lips as she sang about a love that sought her in the hidden corners of the universe. The song was a whisper of hope amidst the darkness, a declaration that even in her solitude, love would find her someday. The chorus echoed like a mantra, a promise she made to herself: 'I know you're somewhere out there, and I know you hear my pain, our paths will come together.'

Her hopes were a reflection in the mirror of the song. In the notes that flowed from her guitar, she imagined a life of love and joy. With her eyes closed, she saw the vision of a shared future: marriage, children's laughter, adventures woven with golden threads of happiness. It was a world she built with every chord, a reality taking shape in the words and melodies flowing from her being.

Even in the most intimate moments, in the solitude of her bathroom, Felipa found an escape. Before the mirror, her lips met the reflection that looked at her with hopeful eyes. She kissed the glass as if she were kissing the love she had not yet found, as if her lips could penetrate the veil of time and space.

She prepared her recorder and began to record. This was the song:

Somewhere

I know it's you, the love of my life
And you're out there somewhere, waiting for me
I don't know you, I can't even imagine what you're like
But in your face, I can draw, calling me

In the distance, you'll hear
I'm calling you from here
Today I'd like to find you
Please, calm my suffering
I know you're somewhere out there
Today, we'll finally coincide
Our paths will merge
It's our story to live

I'm in search of the love of my life
Destiny will help me, I'll find you
And if destiny dares to deny me the chance
Don't worry, my love, I'll wait for you here in eternity

In the distance, you'll hear
I'm calling you from here
Today I'd like to find you
Please, calm my suffering
I know you're somewhere out there
Today, we'll finally coincide
Our paths will merge

It's our story to live

In the distance, you'll hear
I'm calling you from here
Today I'd like to find you
Please, calm my suffering
I know you're somewhere out there
Today, we'll finally coincide
Our paths will merge
It's our story to live

Words flowed like a river in Felipa's mind, an ode to hope and the love she believed she was destined for. In each chord, in every verse, she left a part of herself, a promise that she would keep searching, keep waiting, with the certainty that somehow, her love would find her.

Outside, the sun had vanished. Felipa knew that facing the darkness was inevitable. Anticipation, a painful echo reverberating within her, was a double-edged sword, for the fear of the unknown was often more distressing than the encounter itself.

Anxiety grew like a fire fed by her thoughts, threatening to consume her. Every breath was a conscious effort, an attempt to control the turbulence raging inside her. Fear clung to her bones like an unwelcome intruder with no intention of leaving.

The night advanced, marked by the inexorable ticking of the clock. Like a warrior on the threshold of battle, Felipa fought to stay awake, resisting the call of sleep that was both a refuge and a trap.

Finally, sleep enveloped her, a blanket that seemed to embrace and drag her down into the soft dark. The arrival of the

Nahual, marked by the smell of sulfur, was like a chilling wind seeping through the cracks of her consciousness. In those moments, she called for help from her sister Celeste, a connection that transcended the boundaries between life and death.

The Nahual wore shifting masks, a gallery reflecting the diversity of her fears and nightmares. That night, the face hidden behind a dog mask seemed like an echo of her own vulnerability, a constant reminder that in her struggle, she also faced aspects of herself she preferred not to see.

Immobilized by fear, her eyes clenched shut, she murmured words of supplication that rose like prayers in the silent night. The possession of the Nahual was like a trance in which her will was a prisoner in a macabre dance.

Time lost its meaning amid the whirlwind of emotions and sensations. The clock's hands seemed to stop, and Felipa was dragged into a world of nightmares without limits. Her memories and identity were consumed by the maelstrom of the experience, a battle that left invisible scars on her soul.

When dawn eventually came, it brought its own challenges. Exhausted, Felipa roused herself. The morning ritual, with Nana María's loving assistance, became a dance of masks that hid the struggle raging within her. She dressed herself, with effort, to face the outside world.

Her steps led her to school, accompanied by three classmates blithely unaware of the dark side that inhabited her mind. To them, Felipa seemed like just another schoolgirl, a promising future stretching out before her. However, in the school hallways and beneath her classmates' smiles, a question lingered. Why was Felipa absent so often? It was a puzzle that generated whispers and inquisitive glances. If only they knew the weight of the nights on her shoulders, if they could see the battles she fought in the darkness of her room.

Each of us is like a triptych, with three dimensions of life. One, the public, a mask we show to the world; another, the private, which we only share with those closest to us; and the third, the secret, a hidden part that only we know. Felipa was a perfect example of this trinity, a young woman whose smiling face concealed an internal conflict that tore at her soul.

Yet even if they had known the truth, madness, a term that conceals the complexity of human minds, would be the hasty judgment of those who haven't experienced the dark night of the soul. Because it's not the same to see life from darkness as it is under the bright sun. It's not the same to live through the torment of sleepless nights as it is to observe from the outside. And so, in that duality of the visible and the invisible, Felipa's life was woven like a tapestry of contradictions and internal struggles, a narrative that only she could fully comprehend.

As she walked to school that morning, Felipa glimpsed Cirilo Flores, a peculiar character who often wandered the marketplace. Cirilo's demeanor, cleverly feigned, suggested a fictitious captivity, as if invisible forces were pulling him in a game of appearances; his figure moved in a tug-of-war synchronized by a rider on horseback who seemed possessed by the laughter of the wind.

Cirilo's street theater unfolded like a comedic puppet dance, a choreography of exaggerations that captured the attention of those who crossed his path. However, when Felipa's eyes met Cirilo's, a stirring of intuition diverted her course. As if the shadow of an omen had touched her, she veered in the opposite direction. Yet even as she did, she could not help glancing over her shoulder.

Cirilo's scene seemed torn from a madman's fable, but in that fleeting encounter, Felipa glimpsed something beyond appearances. Her mind opened in an instant, allowing her to pierce the veil of reality, to observe the cracks in the facade of normality. Even if only for a blink, she caught Cirilo's gaze, a gaze that sparkled with flashes of a distorted consciousness. Madness and lucidity danced alongside one another in his eyes, creating an unsettling mosaic.

Words were not necessary to express her perception. She didn't get carried away by the act, didn't fall into the shallowness of the spectacle. Instead, her steps led her down a different path, away from Cirilo's staged comedy. And as she moved forward, a feeling of compassion welled up within her. The figure that appeared to most as a source of laughter, a subject for mockery, was also a human being, a soul that had fallen into the interstices of reality, where the boundaries between judgment and understanding blurred.

The community, with its merciless judgments, had labeled Cirilo the 'town fool.' But in that moment, Felipa saw beyond the label printed by the townsfolk's lazy tongues. Her thoughts accompanied him with a touch of empathy, understanding that loneliness and illness had woven a layer of alternative reality in his mind.

Thus, in the streets of the town, where the facades of normality often conceal the deep currents of existence, Felipa witnessed the fragility of perception. That brief encounter left an impression on her mind, a mark she would remember every time she looked beyond appearances and ventured into the labyrinths of human understanding.

Another day unfurled its monotonous wings at school. Hours slipped heavily by, as if time itself were dragging heavy chains behind it. In the hallways, faces melded into a sea of indifference. Words, time and again, took on hollow forms, like empty seashells dragged along the shore. Life at school seemed like an endless loop, replaying the same scenes over and over. Amidst the crowd, she questioned the purpose of this repetitive existence and clung to the hope that there was something beyond these walls and familiar faces.

After the walk back home, the table was set, the aroma of food filled the air, but Felipa felt no hunger. Nana María's words rose as a constant murmur, highlighting the thinness that had become a mirror of her internal struggle. Food, once a source of pleasure and nourishment, had become another battle.

Following the feast of complaints, Felipa retreated to her room, where homework and the guitar awaited. The routine unfolded like an ancient scroll, written with the same letters day after day. Music, her solace, was like a gentle breeze caressing her weary skin. In the strings of her guitar, she found the freedom to express what words often couldn't convey.

That afternoon, a new song began to take shape, a melody that resonated with the beats of her heart. The notes were a silent declaration of her yearnings, a timid protest against the invisible chains that confined her. The acoustic guitar, like an ally in this internal battle, spoke a language that only Felipa understood.

The song was in its early stages, however, it already carried the weight of her dreams and the burden of her struggles. The title formed in her mind, like a jewel gleaming in the darkness. Each chord, each lyric, was a silent testimony of her resilience, a melody that lifted her spirit above the monotony and reminded her that, despite the challenges, she had the power to create beauty amidst adversity. And so, despite her fatigue, Felipa readied her recorder.

The Theory of Love

Though I've always searched
I never found it
Now that you're here, teach me
What is love? I want to know
Is it something you ask for or something you give?
Can you explain to me the theory of love
because it's something I've never been able to reach?

Na, na, na, na, na, na, na, na, na, na.

For a long time, I waited for it
I won't lose it now
Now that you've come to me, teach me
Is it something that comes to me or do I have to seek it?
Can it be felt? Or can it be touched?
Can you explain to me the theory of love
because it's something I've never been able to reach?

What is love? I want to know
Is it something you ask for or something you give?
Can you explain to me the theory of love
because it's something I've never been able to reach

The nocturnal curtain descended, and in the confines of her room, Felipa completed her musical composition, an act of creation that allowed her to cling to wakefulness until the last trace of energy. Notes and words intertwined into a symphony of emotions, a fleeting respite before facing the dance with insomnia once more. The clock whispered. She had fought, but the inevitable could no longer be delayed.

That night, water took the spotlight. Standing on the shore, beneath the silvery moonlight, Felipa saw herself as a tiny figure in the vastness of the ocean. The sand and the water wove a brief embrace before being dragged apart by the tide.

Each wave was a lament, a struggle in the dance of the current. The ocean's strength was an unrelenting embrace, an abduction she couldn't resist. The waves enveloped her and submerged her into a spiral of fear, a battle for air and solid ground. In that salty embrace, reality blurred, and the night became a symphony of turbulence and distress.

The liquid abyss swallowed her, her body spinning in a ballet of desperation as the sea pulled her deeper. Each meter submerged was a descent into an abyss of darkness and fear. The struggle was in vain, as if the ocean were an unstoppable titan dragging her into the depths.

A silent scream pierced her lips in search of help that never came, a cry in the midst of the sea's silence. Each attempt to breathe was a mute plea, a desperate attempt to return to the surface. Consciousness slowly faded, and in a final flicker of thought, Felipa clung to the memory of her sister Celeste, imagining if she had also felt that terror when the waves carried her to her fateful destiny. And in that ethereal connection, she found a glimmer of solace, knowing that at least her sister's suffering had been fleeting.

The murmur of the sea blended with her last breath, and in the midst of darkness, Felipa plunged into the blackness of the unconscious.

With the first light of dawn, Felipa's eyelids lifted to reveal a new day. However, the cold embrace of reality greeted her with a painful reminder of her nocturnal battle. The bed was damp, soaked with tears and sweat. A wave of shame washed over her, a feeling that sank into her skin and nestled in her heart.

Felipa's instinctive reaction was to hide the evidence of her battle. Like a moving shadow, she covered the bed with the blanket. Each fold of the fabric seemed like another layer to hide her vulnerability, a mask to shield herself from the judgment she feared. She changed her clothes in the darkness of her room, as if she could shed her own skin and leave behind the marks of her internal struggle.

The fear of Nana María's reaction loomed like a dark cloud on the horizon. The emotional scars her father had etched into her heart still burned, and the shame of wetting the bed echoed those painful moments from her childhood. But in the deepest corner of her being, she knew she couldn't let fear and shame rule her. Despite the scars, she was a warrior, a fighter in a battle that transcended wet sheets.

The memory of her father's taunts resonated like a bitter echo. He, who should have been her protector, had become her emotional tormentor. His cruel words were like blades that cut through the innocence of her heart. Though years had passed, the wounds remained open, and the scars were a constant reminder of his cruelty.

In the sands of memory, her father's footprints mingled with the tears of her own struggles. In a twist of fate, Felipa found herself facing a new battle against the bed's dampness, not as a vulnerable child but as a young woman longing to overcome the demons of the past.

Thus, as she faced the day with dampness still present in her bed and in her heart, Felipa became the protagonist of her own story. Every drop of shame mixed with a pinch of courage, every emotional scar became a push to fight against the shadows. Although the battles were internal and often invisible, she was a determined warrior, ready to confront her fears and find beauty in her vulnerability.

After breakfast, fatigue settled on her like a heavy cloak. The simple act of opening her eyes required a titanic effort, and the lazy shadows of the night clung to her mind, refusing to give way to the day. The idea of facing school seemed an epic feat, an odyssey that required every ounce of willpower in her exhausted being. Nana María's gentle yet firm voice echoed in her mind, reminding her of the importance of attendance and the responsibilities weighing on her shoulders. The promise of education was a distant lighthouse, a light guiding her path through the fog of exhaustion.

Every step towards school seemed like a struggle against gravity itself. Her feet dragged wearily, as if she were walking through deep water. Each movement was an effort, a constant reminder that her strength was waning. Her classmates, unaware of her struggle, moved forward in the relentless rhythm of routine.

In the classrooms, time seemed to stretch like elastic, the clock's hands advancing at the pace of a sigh. Her energy and attention, once boundless, had dissipated into the haze of fatigue. The teachers' words reached her ears as a distant murmur, as if the real world existed on a different plane.

Back home, the meal was not a revitalizing balm. Bites slid down her throat at the same dragging pace as time in the classroom, and fatigue continued its exhausting dance in her body. However, homework and tasks did not wait, and she immersed herself in them with what remained of her energy.

The guitar, like a silent confidant, awaited her. Notes flowed from her fingers like melodic thoughts, and lyrics took shape in her mind, like brushstrokes on a blank canvas. Songs were whispered in the vibrations of the strings, as if each chord were a page in the diary of her soul.

So, in the loom of her days, Felipa continued to weave her existence, intertwining moments of struggle and flashes of creativity into a vibrant and complex tapestry. Every chord, every note, every step forward were threads that formed part of her personal narrative, a story of courage amidst fatigue. Although Felipa didn't quite know how to whistle, this song required a whistle in the introduction, so she spent hours learning to whistle until she could do it justice.

The Life I Was Born to Live

A new day has dawned for me
The sun envelops and cradles me in its light
How lucky I am to be what I am
And to be surrounded by so much emotion

I felt very fortunate
To live in fullness
God has given me this life
and I receive it with gratitude

The whole world revolves around me
I set out to conquer my great dreams
And setbacks will teach me
That in this life, I must continue

And I learned to be more human
And to live with my devotion
I discovered that the most sacred thing
Is the joy of being happy

Felipa's melodies were like leaves in the wind, carrying with them stories and emotions that intertwined with the invisible threads of destiny. She composed not only to heal her own wounded heart but also for those who crossed her path. One of them was Carlitos, a brave soul facing an uncertain journey with determination and love.

Felipa's thoughts drifted to the marketplace. In her mind's eye, ahead of her, like a character in a scene, walked Carlitos with a suitcase in hand. The suitcase held not only his belongings but also his mother's dreams and hopes for a better future. Though he was small, his spirit was great.

The curious voices of the townsfolk rose in the air: 'Where are you going, Carlitos?' And he, with the honesty of a pure heart, responded with words that were more than just an answer. They were a song of love and sacrifice, a promise of hard work and unwavering determination.

Felipa walked in silence alongside him, bearing witness to the scene unfolding before her eyes. The marketplace, usually filled with voices and colors, now seemed to be the setting for an intimate moment between mother and son. Carlitos reached his mother's stall, and the words they shared were like a dialogue that transcended time and space. Farewells, dreams, and promises intertwined in a corner of the market, as if the world had paused to make room for the emotion of the moment.

Felipa watched in admiration at Carlitos' unwavering love for his mother. In a world where struggle wore down the human spirit, he was willing to cross borders and defy adversities to ensure his mother's well-being. It was a display of love that touched the deepest fibers of Felipa's heart, a silent lesson in bravery and sacrifice that couldn't be ignored.

That night, as stars painted the sky with their light, Felipa sat with her guitar, seeking to give voice to the emotions she had experienced during the day. The notes flowed like rivers of feeling, and the words intertwined into a song that honored Carlitos' bravery. Each stanza was a tribute to his audacious spirit, his unconditional love, and his unbreakable determination. The melody carried with it the echo of his resolute steps and the promise of a brighter future.

The song reflected the boy whose courage had left a mark on Felipa's heart. It celebrated not only Carlitos but also all those who faced adversity with courage and love in their hearts. Every note was a recognition of the beauty that exists in the anonymous stories of everyday life, an invitation to listen to the hidden melodies in the hearts of those who walk beside us on this journey called life. She turned on the recorder and prepared to record.

Carlitos' Song

Carlitos packed his suitcase, he's leaving now
Walking through the neighborhood, bidding farewell
Curious onlookers wonder as he passes by
'Where is Carlitos going, so determined?'

His mother sells at the market; he's going to fetch her
Mother, I don't want you to work or suffer more
With many children to support and no father around
Money is not enough to provide

I'm leaving for the other side; I'm going to work
I'm going to earn money and help my mother
I'm leaving with the guys, tonight we depart
We'll cross the border, just two more days to go

Mother, I don't want you to suffer, don't cry anymore
I'll send you lots of money; you'll want for nothing
And his mother lifts him up and starts to kiss him
Carlitos is five years old and already a true man

I'm leaving for the other side; I'm going to work
I'm going to earn money and help my mother
And his mother lifts him up and starts to kiss him
Carlitos is five years old and already a true man

The stories of noble hearts are often woven with threads of compassion and selfless acts, and Carlitos, at just five years old with a soul full of determination, embodied this truth in every gesture. His desire to cross borders to work and support his mother resonated like a symphony of sacrifice and love, a melody that transcended his tender years.

Christmas, a time that awakens joy and anticipation in the hearts of children, also touched Carlitos from the doorway of his home. His eyes, like windows to his dreams, watched the play and laughter of his friends while holding a note of sadness inside. Felipa, with her empathetic heart and observant eyes, captured the scene in her mind and heart, feeling the need to fill the void in Carlitos' soul.

The modest Christmas tree, made from a branch of a tree and wrapped in cotton, stood as a symbol of humility and hope at

Carlitos' doorstep. Without glittering ornaments or lavish gifts, it was a testament to the simplicity of his life and the greatness of his spirit. That bare tree seemed to whisper a story of struggle and dreams, a narrative that Felipa listened to attentively.

Felipa's decision to act arose as an echo of compassion within her. She took money from her own savings and headed to the market. Amidst the colorful offerings and the hustle and bustle of the people, she chose a simple toy truck. She wrapped it in newspaper, a layer of affection that concealed the treasure within, and made her way to Carlitos' door, carrying a promise of happiness with her.

The gift-giving was a moment of magic in the midst of simplicity. Felipa's words, spoken with gentleness, made Carlitos' eyes sparkle like stars in the night. The gift, though modest, carried within it Felipa's generosity and affection, a demonstration that love could manifest in the simplest and most genuine actions.

That scene, like a painting frozen in time, resonated in Felipa's heart and became the inspiration for another song. The melody told the story of a gift that transcended its materiality, a gift far greater than a simple toy truck. It was a reflection of Felipa's love and empathy, a song that paid tribute to the power of touching lives with small, heartfelt gestures.

Each note was a promise that love and compassion could illuminate even the darkest corners of life. It was a tribute to Carlitos and all those whose stories, like stars in the firmament, left a bright mark on the canvas of existence. And as the strings vibrated with the melody, the echo of that special day in the marketplace became a song that transcended time and space. Her recorder helped her immortalize those magical moments.

Empty Christmas Tree

I've written you some letters, and you haven't been able to reply
I longed eagerly for your arrival at Christmas
You forgot about me, you didn't bring my toys
You forgot about me, you shattered my illusion
He and I, an empty Christmas tree
He and I, as sad as Christmas
He and I, an empty Christmas tree
He and I, as cold as Christmas

The children all over the neighborhood are very happy, playing outside
My hands are empty; I couldn't reach a toy
You forgot about me, you didn't bring my toys
You forgot about me, you shattered my illusion
He and I, an empty Christmas tree
He and I, as sad as Christmas
He and I, an empty Christmas tree
He and I, as cold as Christmas

At night, when I go to bed, a tear must fall
It's not fair that the poorest ones always suffer the most
You forgot about me, you didn't bring my toys
You forgot about me, you shattered my illusion
He and I, an empty Christmas tree
He and I, as sad as Christmas
He and I, an empty Christmas tree
He and I, as cold as Christmas

The night descended upon the world like a dark and mysterious cloak, and with it came the inevitable encounter with the mirror, a reflection of her own existence that became more unsettling with each meeting. On this night, like so many others, Felipa wrestled against the embrace of sleep, resisting the creeping fatigue that threatened to pull her into unconsciousness. But, like waves finally yielding to the shore, her resistance gave way, and she sank into the arms of slumber.

The dream mirror cast not just a physical reflection but exposed Felipa's vulnerability, her inner struggles and weaknesses. The mirror, radiating a cruel clarity, presented her life in all its minutiae, revealing the dark corners that Felipa preferred to hide even from herself. It was as if each fragment of the mirror were a window to her own soul, unveiling layers of her being that had remained hidden in the shadows of denial.

The image reflected back by the mirror was not one she wished to see. The mirror showed her selfishness, doubts, and fears, pictures that were difficult to confront. Anger grew within her, a burning flame fueled by frustration and self-reproach. She grabbed a stone, an instrument of her own discontent, and hurled it at the mirror, as if aiming not at the glass, but the reflection of herself that it contained.

The sound of shattering glass filled the air, a symphony of release and chaos. Shards of the mirror fell to the floor, each carrying a part of her reflection, a piece of her fractured identity. Fissures extended like cracks in ice, splitting her image in two, then more, until her reflection became a kaleidoscope of distorted and disconnected shapes. It was as if her soul had split into countless fragments, each expressing a different part of her being.

Desperate, Felipa tried to gather up the pieces of the mirror, as if she could reassemble her shattered identity. But the fragments were too numerous. Each attempt to put them back together only resulted in a multiplication of cracks and fractures.

From there, the night turned into a maze of shadows, her own identity lost among the shattered glimmers of the mirror. Fear enveloped her like a cold wind. She longed to find her way back to herself, but on that dark night, her steps were uncertain, her internal compass spinning uselessly.

Yet, amid the shadows of despair, a glimmer of light remained, a small but persistent spark of hope that resisted being extinguished. That fragile yet enduring spark held the possibility of a day when the broken pieces might find a way to come together again. In that hope lay the promise that, though the current night was clouded by confusion and bewilderment, someday the fragments could be reassembled to form a complete picture of the strong and resilient woman Felipa was destined to be.

The day began with its relentless routine, burdened by a night of inner struggle. Felipa rose from her bed as if dragging behind her the weight of the nighttime hours she had spent facing her own demons. The act of getting dressed, once automatic and effortless, was now a slow and meticulous task. Each garment seemed to be an additional layer of the fatigue that overwhelmed her. Felipa sometimes wondered what she would have to do for Nana María to listen and truly believe in the existence of the four nocturnal entities that tortured her without mercy.

The mirror in the corner of her room looked at her with the same unrelenting clarity she had experienced in her dreams. The eyes in the reflection were dark with shadows.

On her way to school, she walked like a shade among the others, concealing the pain she carried within. Her classmates chatted as if nothing was wrong. She clung to the hope that someday she could overcome all the difficulties and live fully, like the girls she walked beside but each day that passed without relief felt like a painful reminder of how far she was from that goal.

School was a temporary refuge from her tormenting thoughts. Although every day was a struggle to stay focused on the lessons, the time in the classrooms provided her with a respite from the nightly battles and a momentary distraction from her inner pain. But even amidst the classrooms filled with classmates and teachers, a sense of isolation surrounded her, as if she were trapped in a bubble of her own suffering.

Returning home after school, she faced a new set of challenges. The food on her plate tasted bland, and though Nana María tried to ensure she ate enough, her lack of appetite was only a physical manifestation of her emotional exhaustion. Still, she forced herself to eat. She knew she had to continue, that every day of struggle was a step toward the possible liberation from her torment. She searched for cracks in the armor of despair, seeking a way to overcome the obstacles that prevented her from living the life she longed for.

So she continued, day by day, night by night, battle by battle. She knew there were no easy answers or instant solutions, but she was willing to face whatever was necessary to find her way to healing and redemption. With each morning that dawned, she carried with her the hope that someday the doors that had tormented her for so long would open to a life of peace, fulfillment, and happiness.

That afternoon, the sky seemed to have painted itself with a deeper and more tranquil blue, as if nature itself joined the procession that moved solemnly through the streets of Agua Fría. Felipa leaned over the balcony of her house, her eyes met the sea of people filling the streets with devotion and faith in their hearts. She had never witnessed such a vast congregation in her small town, a blend of locals and pilgrims who came from distant regions like Puebla and Veracruz.

Whispers of prayer and religious songs floated in the air, like collective sighs lifted toward the divine. And then, like a vision of purity and grace, the Virgin of the Dump appeared on a float adorned with white flowers, pulled by a humble donkey that moved with calm and solemn steps. The radiant white of her dress contrasted with the simplicity of the procession, but there was no room for discord in that sacred moment.

Felipa's weary eyes grew wide with astonishment at the sight of the Virgin of the Dump. She felt as if time had stood still, as if her entire world had concentrated in that moment. It was more than an image; it was a symbol of hope and comfort, a tangible representation of all the longings deep within her heart. That morning, astride her float, the Virgin of the Dump encapsulated all the qualities Felipa wished for in her life: peace, love, harmony, and humility.

A murmur of admiring sighs rippled through the crowd as the Virgin threw a handful of red petals into the air. One of them found its way to Felipa's cheek, a gentle touch that seemed to hold the promise of something more. With trembling hands and a rapidly beating heart, she picked it up reverently and brought it to her lips, leaving a tender kiss filled with emotions she couldn't fully comprehend.

An overwhelming feeling filled her being, and tears flowed without restraint. Her cheeks moistened as emotion flooded over her. It was as if that petal had been the key that unlocked a torrent of suppressed feelings, a relief that manifested in every tear. In that moment, she felt as though an invisible burden had lifted from her shoulders, releasing her from a weight she had scarcely recognized she carried.

The Virgin of the Dump looked upwards, and her eyes met Felipa's, a connection that transcended words and rational explanations. In that silent exchange, Felipa could feel the deep and empathetic understanding of the Virgin. She watched as the Virgin's eyes moved over her hands, pausing at her battered and wounded nails, an external manifestation of the internal battles she faced every night. And then, like an echo in her mind, the words of the Virgin of the Dump resounded: 'You must face your fears.'

It was as if the Virgin had read her darkest thoughts, had sensed her insecurities and pain, and with her gaze and those words, offered her silent guidance toward liberation. Felipa felt exposed and, at the same time, understood. She knew there was a path she had to take, a path of confrontation and overcoming, a path that could lead her to the healing she so desperately craved.

The procession flowed on, carrying the Virgin with it, but leaving in Felipa's heart a seed of transformation. She withdrew from the balcony, a spark of determination in her eyes. She knew the road ahead wouldn't be easy, that facing her fears would be a daunting and challenging task, but for the first time in a long time, she felt her internal compass cease its aimless spinning and point the way forward.

Felipa watched the procession recede, a sense of gratitude and hope filling her heart. The tide of emotions that had invaded her during that encounter clung to her throughout the rest of the day, as if she had been touched by something divine and sacred. The Virgin had left an indelible mark on her soul, an imprint that urged her to do something more with her life, to confront the internal demons that had haunted her nights and days.

That afternoon, a creative impulse overcame her. She sat down with her guitar and let her fingers dance over the strings, giving life to a melody that resonated with the vibration of her revitalized spirit. The song that emerged from her heart had an intriguing title: Kill Them Quietly. The words came as an echo from her mind, a call to action she didn't fully understand but seemed to emanate from a place deep within her.

The song took shape and became a tale of sadness and despair. The young protagonist was a reflection of her own internal struggles, a misunderstood and tormented figure facing the judgment of her small town. Through the lyrics and the notes, Felipa brought the story of that young woman to life, capturing her emotions in every chord and verse.

Although the song was imbued with deep sadness, it also carried a nuance of resistance and courage. Creating it became a liberating act for Felipa. Every word, every chord was a step toward expressing her own struggles and fears. It was her voice rising against the darkness that had invaded her life, a way of telling the world that she wouldn't be silenced by her inner demons or by the criticisms of those who didn't understand her suffering.

Writing this song filled her with a renewed sense of purpose. It became her personal battle cry, the soundtrack of her struggle to find light in the midst of darkness. It gave her the strength and determination to confront the fears that had haunted her for so long. Felipa understood that the time had come to free herself from the chains that had kept her from living her life.

The song became a constant reminder of her inner strength, a beacon of hope guiding her toward authenticity and redemption. Every time she touched the guitar strings and let the words flow, she felt closer to finding her way to healing and wholeness. The song wasn't just a piece of music; it was a testament to her resilience and a commitment to her own transformation.

And so, with the song as her guide, Felipa began to walk a path of self-discovery and empowerment. Each day, she faced her fears with renewed determination, inspired by the strength she had found within herself and in the presence of the Virgin of the Dump. The procession of her life continued, yet now, she was determined to lead it with courage and authenticity, writing her own story rather than letting her fears dictate the narrative.

The darkness of the night enveloped Felipa as she mentally prepared to confront her greatest fear. No more evasions, no more running away. She was determined to confront her tormentor, to unmask the being that had haunted her night after night. She curled up in her bed, closing her eyes with determination and ready to stay conscious despite the invading fear.

The hours seemed endless as she waited, battling sleep and anxiety. Finally, exhaustion overcame her, and her eyes closed. However, this time her sleep was not marked by passivity; she was prepared to challenge whatever came. And then, she felt its sinister presence materializing behind her. The smell of sulfur filled the air, but Felipa didn't back down. This time, she wouldn't allow it.

The Nahual appeared, his face covered by a cow's mask. Felipa felt his hands on her body, and though terror pulsed within her, she remembered her purpose. With fierce determination, she snatched the mask from the Nahual and threw it to the ground. The monster that had stalked her for so long was exposed, but what she saw left her breathless and with her heart in her throat.

Before her stood Benjamín, her father's best friend. The man who should have been a protector, a confidant, turned out to be the Nahual, her nighttime abuser. Felipa's world rocked at that moment; all certainties turned into doubts, and everything she had trusted crumbled. Anger and betrayal mingled within her, creating a storm of emotions threatening to engulf her.

In her search for answers and solace, she ran to her father's room, yet her father lay in bed, drunk, oblivious to his daughter's emotional turmoil. Felipa's world teetered even further; the sense of abandonment and hopelessness solidified in her heart.

She ran from the room, tears in her eyes and her heart shattered into a thousand pieces. Deception, betrayal, and violence had invaded every corner of her life. Her own home had become a nightmare, where those who should protect her were the ones hurting her. She felt desolate, exposed, a young woman trapped in a spiral of pain and mistrust. But before she could gather herself, the next challenge appeared.

It was the mirror of her life, which once reflected her dreams and aspirations but was now shattered, just like her trust in the world around her. However, in the midst of the darkness, a spark of determination and inner strength ignited in Felipa. She knew she couldn't allow despair to consume her entirely. Though her life lay in ruins, she clung to the hope of finding a path to healing and redemption.

With a heart filled with pain and newfound courage, Felipa knew she had to confront her past and seek a better future. Despite closed doors and the nightmares that haunted her, she was determined to open a new door to the light. With each step, she sought truth, strength, and the courage to rewrite her story and transform her life into one of resilience and triumph.

She had faced the Nahual, and stared down the mirror. Now it was time to challenge the water. She ran to the Tepetate River, it's dark surface stretching before her like a mirror of her inner struggle. The night embraced her with its mystery as she immersed herself in the water, wading in deep, feeling worries and pain begin to dissipate. Amidst the current, her body floated in the river's embrace, slowly spinning as the water caressed her. She had practiced that moment thousands of times in her dreams, and now she made it a reality.

Time became elastic, and while trembling from the cold water, a sense of liberation washed over her. She felt like a chrysalis breaking free from its confines, emerging with newfound strength. In her mind echoed the words, 'I am free from all fears!' Every heartbeat, every movement in the water affirmed her triumph over the oppression of fear. 'Fear, you die, I live!' she whispered with euphoria as the river closed her in its icy embrace.

The next challenge, the final trial to face, was the most daunting of all: the door. With resolute eyes, she observed the entrance to her nightly terrors and finally crossed its threshold.

At dawn, she rode alongside a black-clad charro on the banks of the Tepetate River. In the distance, her father, immersed in incomprehensible pain, held something in his arms as tears welled up in his eyes. She couldn't comprehend his agony because, in that moment, Felipa was infused with a peace she had longed for. Crossing the door was the path to true serenity.

The emotions that had tormented her seemed to have evaporated, like the morning mist dispersing with the first rays of the sun. Her heartbeat echoed with constant tranquility, and the anxieties and panic attacks had been replaced by the simple joy of 'being.' From a distance, she bid farewell to her father, a farewell laden with love and a message echoing in the wind: 'I love you, I'll miss you.'

In the arms of the black-clad charro, embracing the peace she had found, Felipa felt the joy of having crossed the door that finally opened for her. The other doors remained closed, reminders of the challenges she had faced and overcome. There was no opportunity to open other doors, but that didn't matter. The only door that opened for her, the one inviting her to enter, was the door that showed her the reality of her life. It was the door she had chosen to cross, without fear and at peace with herself. Because the only door that opened for her was the door of suicide.

Kill Them Silently

Lying on a bed of roses, with gestures reflecting profound peace
You finally found the eternal light, as your angelic face proclaims
Tired of living in this world, you chose to visit the beyond
I, hidden amidst the murmurs of people who judge you mercilessly
Silence yourselves! Silence, all of you! Who are you to pass judgment?

Understand, respect the mourning and the pain in this home
She's defenseless now, unable to answer your accusations
If she were awake, you wouldn't dare to speak

The church bells toll, and we slowly traverse the city
I endure the gazes of people who point fingers with unjust reproach
I wonder what your life would have been like if I could have rescued you in time
I carry a heavy burden of guilt in my soul for not being there in your darkest moment
Silence yourselves! Silence, all of you! Who are you to pass judgment?
Understand, respect the mourning and the pain in this home
She's defenseless now, unable to answer your accusations
If she were awake, you wouldn't dare to speak

Author's Note

Suicide is real. We must believe our loved ones when they tell us they are depressed or have suicidal thoughts. They are crying out for help, and we should not abandon them.

Jaime Goicoechea Zúñiga is the author and composer of all the songs in this book.
© Copyright 2023

All songs are performed by Hermanos Sanromán.
Album: La ley del Mexicano.
Available on all music platforms.

The Virgin of the Dump

I approached you and felt serenity. I touched your mantle and received peace. I looked into your eyes and discovered love. I kissed your hand and sensed your mercy. You touched my head, and I saw your grace. You embraced me, and I believed in your protection. I cried in your arms and heard your blessings. I thanked you, and your purity deeply moved me. With your smile, all my troubles vanished.

Pompeya, a woman of indomitable spirit and a compassionate heart, went about her daily routine on her way to the Agua Fría recycling center. From the early hours of the morning, the sun rose above the horizon, illuminating the picturesque town and highlighting the unique beauty of each street and lane. Pompeya, however, walked through the gleaming dawn with a purpose: to sell the cans and corrugated cardboard she diligently collected from the local dump.

The residents of Agua Fría admired Pompeya's determination. While some might have seen her task as a mere act of survival, others recognized in her a deep sense of environmental responsibility and an unbreakable will to improve her community.

Pushing the two-wheeled cart that had become her faithful companion, Pompeya made her way through the cobbled streets of the town. Her pack of dogs followed closely, as if they understood the importance of her mission. Five canines of different sizes and colors, each with their own personality, accompanied her everywhere, displaying a loyalty that transcended words.

97

The undisputed leader of the pack was named Canelo. A canine with a reddish coat, his strength was admirable. His muscles seemed sculpted by nature itself, and his fiery gaze reflected unwavering determination. Canelo faced any adversary that crossed his path with daring courage. He was the children's hero, a fierce guardian, and a constant source of amazement. After school, kids would stop and watch in awe as Canelo took on even three dogs at once, defeating them with a combination of agility and strategy. He had earned a place in everyone's heart as a true warrior, a living emblem of courage and determination.

The second member of the pack was Sandungo, a name given to him in honor of Pompeya's favorite song, 'La Sandunga.' Sandungo, unlike Canelo, stood out for his clumsiness and his easily distracted nature. However, there was something special about him: his unwavering devotion to Pompeya. When she got angry and her stick came out for punishment, all the dogs would flee at top speed to avoid it, except Sandungo. He stood firm, ready to take the blow instead of abandoning his beloved owner. His loyalty was a lesson in unconditional love and resilience in the face of adversity.

La Coqueta was a spirited little female dog. Her streetwise nature often led her to wander away from the pack for days, exploring the corners of the town. Yet, as if guided by a magnet, she always returned to Pompeya's home, bringing stories of her solitary adventures and explorations.

Laika, the matriarch of the pack, was a being worthy of veneration. It was she who had given birth to the others. Her protective maternal instinct and canine wisdom made her the spiritual guide of the pack, ensuring that each one found their place in this world where human and canine lives met and intertwined.

Lastly, there was Benito, a medium-sized black dog with intelligence that defied all expectations. Pompeya used to say with a smile, 'If that dog could talk, he'd be the president of Mexico.' Benito, whose name honored Don Benito Juárez, one of Mexico's most notable leaders, had a discerning gaze that seemed to understand the secrets of the universe.

And so, with Canelo, Sandungo, La Coqueta, Laika, and Benito by her side, Pompeya walked the streets of Agua Fría, not just as a waste picker but as a leader in the world of stray dogs and a teacher in the school of life. The pack was more than a group of canines; they were a family united by bonds of love and respect, a community that demonstrated that, in loyalty and companionship, even the most disadvantaged could find purpose and a profound sense of belonging.

Pompeya had woven her life into the mysteries and secrets of the municipal dump and left her mark in that seemingly desolate place for two decades. Her dwelling, a makeshift construction crafted from salvaged wood and corrugated cardboard, stood as a silent testament to her ability to transform what others deemed waste into something useful and dignified. The passage of time only solidified her position in that unconventional corner; no one objected to her presence, and so it was that Pompeya, with the simplicity of her determination, established herself in that peculiar home.

The dump, in its paradoxical nature, provided Pompeya with everything she needed to subsist. Cans and corrugated cardboard, which others thought to be useless, were to her vital resources. With these, Pompeya found a source of income, and the need to pursue other work was negated by the abundance of recyclable materials. At fifty-five years old, Pompeya's life was intertwined with that vast and often underestimated realm of waste. Her only companions were her dogs, faithful guardians of her solitary domain, and the very dump that had welcomed and nourished her for so many years.

Inside her unique dwelling, a world of recycled treasures unfolded before curious eyes. A television, a witness to untold stories, and a radio that tuned into the voices of the outside world, stood as the guardians of her thoughts and emotions. The living room and dining room, with furniture constructed from what others had discarded, were a testament to her ability to see beyond the superficial. And in the bedroom, an intimate and personal corner, lay a bed of dreams woven with the fibers of her history.

The exterior of the house was a mosaic of curiosities and potential utilities. From abandoned kitchen utensils to remnants of electronic gadgets, each object had its designated place in that improvised setting. Even a dentist's chair, a symbol of a profession she never thought of practicing, stood as a monument to her adaptability and her ability to find value in the unexpected. Pompeya collected these relics with the discernment of a connoisseur, knowing that, at some point, her life might need them.

And so, in the shadows of the dump, Pompeya wove her story with threads of perseverance and creativity. Her home, a tribute to resilience and authenticity, stood as a beacon amidst a sea of waste. In a world where transformation was at its essence, Pompeya was the embodiment of the human capacity to find beauty and purpose in the most unexpected places.

That day, as the golden sun's rays began to yield to the embrace of twilight, Pompeya embarked on her familiar routine of selling the cans and cardboard she had diligently collected at the recycling center. The coins she received weren't much, but they were enough to keep her small home and feed her beloved pack of dogs.

Upon her return, the air laden with promises of the night, Pompeya prepared to take a well-deserved rest. However, something in the atmosphere seemed different. Soon, her intuition was confirmed when she noticed the absence of Laika, the revered matriarch of her loyal pack. Her heart raced as she scanned the boundaries of the dump in search of her canine companion.

It was then that her gaze fell on an unusual place, in a corner illuminated by the presence of an improvised altar, a place where the Virgin of the Scavengers, like a beacon of faith in the midst of darkness, shone with her spiritual light. But what caught Pompeya's attention was not just the devotional image but the solitary figure of Laika in that place of worship.

'Why would Laika be there?' Pompeya wondered with a gesture of concern that intertwined with the mystery of the moment.

She called Laika, but there was no response. Curious and driven by her unease, Pompeya ventured deeper into the dump, navigating through the mounds of waste in her search. The shroud of night seemed to cast shadows over the enigma before her.

Finally, destiny led her to the threshold of the chapel where the altar of Our Lady of the Scavengers stood. And there, in a moment that stopped her heart's beating, she discovered the object of Laika's attention. A baby, fragile and vulnerable, lay there in a kind of divine embrace, defying all logic and understanding.

Amazement flooded Pompeya, her thoughts and emotions colliding like waves in her mind. 'A baby!' she exclaimed, her voice vibrating with a mixture of astonishment and concern. The words reverberated, mingling with the echo of her thoughts. There was no answer to her rhetorical question, only the raw and bewildering reality of life abandoned on the threshold of the dump.

Pompeya's heartbeat with a mixture of compassion and bewilderment. 'Who could have thought to throw a baby in the dump?' she wondered aloud, incredulity and indignation intertwining in her words.

The mystery stretched before her, shrouded in the darkness of the night and the intermittent light of Our Lady of the Scavengers. And in that instant, Pompeya stood on the threshold of a new odyssey, one that would lead her to explore the mysteries of life, hope, and the human capacity to find beauty in the unexpected.

The sight of the abandoned baby had shaken the foundations of Pompeya's reality, thrusting her into the heart of an unexpected dilemma. Fearful of getting involved in such a delicate matter, her steps took her to the town hall, where the authority and the duty to protect the citizens rested in the hands of the police commander. However, the commander's priorities did not seem to align with the urgency of the moment, as he was more concerned with satisfying his hunger than addressing Pompeya's call for help.

'Commander,' Pompeya began, her voice resonating with a mixture of anguish and determination. 'Someone has thrown a baby into the dump, and the incredible thing is that it's alive!'

Pompeya's eyes searched for a sign of astonishment in the commander, but she found only indifference. The commander, in the midst of chewing his lunch, looked at her with a mix of boredom and annoyance. His response was like a silent slap, undermining the hope and seriousness of the situation.

'Don't talk nonsense,' the commander replied condescendingly. 'No one throws babies away. Maybe the parents forgot him and will come back for him later.'

The commander's words hung in the air, an unrelenting denial of the reality Pompeya had witnessed. She felt helpless in the face of the cold logic that dismissed the inconceivable. The commander's incredulity, far from soothing her concerns, intensified them.

As she left the town hall, Pompeya carried with her a burden of disappointment and bewilderment. She had sought help from the authorities, only to find a closed door of indifference. The need for action drove her to the parish, where she hoped to find compassion and guidance from the priest. However, the irony of fate prevailed, as the priest was absent, dedicated to a labor of love and service in aid of the needy.

Frustration pushed Pompeya to return to the place that had witnessed an unresolved mystery: the altar of the Our Lady of the Scavengers. That place had been a sanctuary of worship and hope, but now it was also the epicenter of overwhelming uncertainty. The baby, abandoned and fragile, was there, in a vulnerable state that called to her sense of compassion and urgency.

Concern for the baby's health motivated her to quicken her pace. As she approached, her heart beat with an anxious rhythm. The scene that unfolded before Pompeya's astonished eyes was like a flash of light in the darkness of the night. Laika, the matriarch of the pack, displayed a maternal instinct that defied expectations and transcended barriers. With touching gentleness, Laika was nursing the baby with her own teat.

The astonishing revelation left Pompeya speechless, her heart beating with a mixture of disbelief and gratitude. Laika's eyes, filled with a kindness that needed no words, met Pompeya's, and in that moment, Pompeya understood that the baby's presence had awakened something profound in Laika's heart, a maternal spark that defied any logical explanation.

Sadness still weighed on Pompeya like a painful shadow. Only two days ago, Laika's puppies had faced a tragic fate, drowned by an unrelenting storm that flooded the place where they rested. That loss had been a devastating blow to Laika, but now, in the midst of the darkness, a new opportunity for love and care was emerging.

The hottest day of the year had arrived; the heat felt like a distillation of the sun itself had been spread across the earth. Pompeya found herself at an unexpected crossroads: the life of a baby depended on her decision. The option of letting the baby face the same fate as Laika's puppies seemed cruel and inconceivable. At that moment, Pompeya made a choice that would change the course of her life.

She decided to take the baby to her home, accepting the challenge of caring for this abandoned little life. The baby became a symbol of hope and renewal, a reminder that even in the midst of tragedy, the opportunity for love and care can arise from the ashes. Pompeya held the baby in her arms with a mixture of anxiety and tenderness, knowing she was taking on an unprecedented responsibility.

The relationship between Laika and the baby was a miracle in itself. Laika continued to nurse the baby with devotion, an act of care that went beyond biology and delved into the depths of the heart. Pompeya watched in amazement as Laika kept bringing her teat to the baby, providing vital sustenance with a gentleness that defied understanding.

As the moon rose, illuminating the darkness with its soft silver light, Pompeya couldn't help but find a hint of humor amidst the wonder of the moment. 'Well,' she commented with a smile that combined surprise and gratitude, 'at least we don't have to spend money on baby formula.'

Her gaze shifted to the baby's diaper, feeling a mixture of anxiety and curiosity. Amidst soft laughter and intertwined emotions, her voice filled the air with a joyful exclamation: 'It's a girl!'

In that moment, amidst starry night and the profound mysteries of the dump, Pompeya experienced a deep connection with Laika and the baby. Laika, the mother of a loving heart, and the baby, a symbol of reborn hope, formed a bond that defied the barriers of nature and reminded Pompeya that, in the most unexpected places, life can flourish with a beauty that transcends understanding.

Two days after discovering the baby in the dump, Pompeya returned to the town hall in search of answers and guidance. Her heart was filled with unease, and her mind had become a whirlwind of thoughts, each laden with concern for the fate of the girl she had given refuge to.

The conversation with the police commander did not offer the reassurance she had hoped for. His words resonated with a mixture of understanding and apathy, as if the gravity of the matter did not correspond to the importance Pompeya attributed to it. The commander's words, though somewhat reassuring, left Pompeya with an uncomfortable feeling. 'No one is going to accuse you of anything, Pompeya. Keep taking care of the girl until her parents claim her,' the commander insisted, his voice tinged with a patience that seemed to blend with the monotony of his work.

The response was not what Pompeya had expected. She was in a moral and emotional dilemma, facing a decision that had the potential to change the course of her days. Concern for the girl's future overwhelmed her, and the idea that the parents might not return filled her with an anxiety she couldn't ignore.

Despite her worries, time passed without anyone coming to resolve the mystery of the abandoned girl. Pompeya found herself in an emotional limbo, caring for the little one with a love that grew with each passing day. The connection between them strengthened with every shared moment, and the idea of parting from the girl began to seem unimaginable.

The girl, once unknown and vulnerable, had become a ray of light in Pompeya's life. The unconditional love that Pompeya had given and received from her dogs expanded to embrace the girl. The little one had become an integral part of her life, a presence that filled her home with laughter and babbling, a presence that defied any preconceived expectations.

As Pompeya watched the girl grow and flourish, she began to consider a decision that would change their lives forever: the idea of adopting her as her own daughter began to take shape in her mind and heart. Although the circumstances were unusual, and society might look upon her decision with suspicion, Pompeya felt that her destiny was intertwined with that of the girl.

One morning, as the sun emerged in its golden splendor, Pompeya made a decision. She consulted the saints' calendar, and her eyes landed on the name of the day: San Felipe. As if a wink from destiny, Pompeya felt a special connection with that name. She decided that it was time to give the girl a name, a name that would carry with it the love and hope that had blossomed in her heart. Thus, Felipa became the tangible embodiment of Pompeya's decision, a name that would be a testament to a new chapter in their intertwined lives.

Laika continued to nurse Felipa until the girl could take her first bites of solid food. As the child grew, Laika and Felipa became playmates and partners in crime, while Pompeya's life, shaped by the darkness and light of the dump, was transformed into a story of resilience, love, and redemption. Her home, a combination of scavenged junk and open hearts, was filled with laughter and joy. And at the center of it all, Pompeya and Felipa, an inseparable duo that defied expectations and reminded everyone that, in the most unexpected places, beauty can emerge, and lives can converge on a path of meaning and purpose.

***

Months passed like leaves carried by the wind, and on the threshold of the dump, the girl known as Felipa grew in deafening silence. No one came to claim her, neither the parents who had left her to fate nor the authorities who seemed blind to her presence. The dump, with its chaotic symphony of waste and secrets, and Pompeya, with her open heart and her home made of recycled memories, were two points lost on the horizon of society, two realities that mattered least in the universe to the rest of the world.

The years passed like chapters of a book whose pages had never been read. The girl grew up in the heart of the dump, a place that became her world and her refuge. Felipa's childhood was a delicate balance between poverty and happiness, a paradox that only those who dared to look beyond appearances could understand.

In the heart of the dump, Felipa discovered a hidden treasure in the shadows. The place became her own storehouse of wonders, a vast world of possibilities where every discarded object held a story. She played with broken dolls, rescuing their beauty and creating new stories for them. Incomplete puzzles came to life under her skillful hands, and toy cars without wheels rolled along imaginary roads that only she could see. Coloring books, already used but still full of potential, became her canvases, each page filled with colors that reflected her vibrant soul.

Life in the dump was marked by simplicity and authenticity. Felipa's laughter blended with the sounds of the wind among the waste, and her joy resonated like a song on a stage seemingly forgotten by the outside world. Pompeya, the maternal and protective figure in Felipa's life, became her guide and friend. Together, they shared moments of learning and growth, weaving memories that would become threads of connection between their hearts.

As the years slid by with the grace of a tranquil river, Felipa and Pompeya's bond grew only stronger. The girl, who had been abandoned in a harsh place, found in the landfill and in Pompeya a family that transcended the bonds of blood. They grew together, like two souls intertwined in a dance of love and care.

Felipa's childhood, though marked by material poverty, was enriched with a spiritual wealth that only those who have known adversity can understand. She learned lessons of gratitude, creativity, and perseverance that are not taught in formal classrooms but in the school of life that only the dump could provide.

Every corner of Pompeya's modest home echoed with creativity and adaptability. Felipa immersed herself in a world of possibilities that transcended their material poverty. In one corner rested a six-drawer dresser, a piece that might seem insignificant at first glance but was, in reality, a treasure trove full of secrets.

The dresser, with its scent of old wood and its patina of forgotten stories, was a chest of treasures that Felipa explored with admiration and gratitude. Each drawer was a portal to a different universe, filled with second-hand clothing that had been rescued and cared for with affection. A large mirror, albeit cracked, stood as a window to the world of possibilities that life could offer. Every morning, Felipa stood before it, combing her hair, her small fingers filled with determination. Despite the imperfections of the mirror, it reflected the image of a girl full of hope and resilience.

The room filled with Felipa's musical laughter as she explored her wardrobe. The variously colored garments and accessories forgotten by others found new life in her creative hands. Felipa indulged in changing her wardrobe according to her whim, experimenting with different combinations. In those moments, she felt like a queen in her own realm, surrounded by comforts that had been rescued from oblivion.

However, among all the wonders of the dump, what fascinated Felipa the most were the books. A stack of books that had been thrown into the trash became her gateway to unknown worlds and thrilling adventures. As she learned to read, every word became a key that opened doors to new horizons of knowledge and exploration. Her favorites were the biographies of those who had left indelible marks on the history of humanity. Gandhi, Buddha, Mother Teresa of Calcutta, Saint John Paul II, Samael

Aun Weor, and Nelson Mandela became constant companions in her thoughts and dreams.

The dump, with its paradox of waste and treasures, continued to be a world of wonder and discovery for Felipa. One day, among the extravagances hidden among the discarded objects, she found garments that were not just clothing but manifestations of identity and creativity. She dared to experiment, and one day, dazzling and bold, she dressed provocatively, wearing a blonde wig that gave her an air of mystery, high-heeled shoes that gave her an imposing stature, and a dress too short for her age.

When Felipa walked through the landfill in high heels, her small and determined figure bent her legs as she walked, imitating the elegance of the models she had only seen in the pages of worn-out magazines. Pompeya, watching the spectacle with affection and amusement, burst into laughter at the sight. In that moment, the landfill became a stage of freedom and self-expression, where even discarded objects could find new meaning, and limitations were only opportunities for Felipa's flourishing creativity.

In the heart of the dump, a connection that transcended words had been forged between Felipa and Laika. Like a protective mother and an adopted daughter, they shared a bond that was deeper than biology itself. Every step Felipa took was accompanied by the reliable silhouette of Laika, a presence that offered comfort and security amid the uncertainty of the world.

Their days were like a blank canvas, waiting to be painted with the vibrant colors of shared joy. They played in the shaded corners of the landfill, where discarded objects became elements of fun and imagination. Felipa's melodious laughter and Laika's playful barks filled the air with contagious energy, a reminder that happiness could be found even in the most unexpected places.

Their complicity knew no bounds. As night fell, when the stars blinked in the sky like bright diamonds, Felipa and Laika shared dreams in the intimacy of their improvised home. The girl's dreams mingled with the moving paws and twitching ears of Laika's sleep, creating a silent dance of shared hopes and wishes.

However, their adventures were not confined to the limits of the landfill. Together, they explored the boundaries of the known world, facing the horizon with bravery and excitement. The Tepetate River, located on the outskirts of Agua Fría, became their secret refuge. It was a place where water flowed with the same serenity as time, and where nature seemed to whisper ancient secrets to the wind.

Felipa and Laika crossed the green fields, their steps filled with anticipation. Upon reaching the Tepetate River, they immersed themselves in the refreshing waters, embracing the feeling of freedom that only water could offer. Felipa's laughter echoed among the trees, and Laika swam with grace and joy, her paws moving in a natural choreography that seemed to lead her to pure happiness.

The passage of years continued to weave the threads of Felipa's life into the tapestry of time. While the sun and the moon shared their eternal dance in the sky, Felipa advanced on her educational path. She was no longer just a child playing among the forgotten treasures of the dump, but a young girl becoming an explorer of knowledge. Pompeya realized that the time had come for Felipa to step out into the wider world.

Though she had missed the first grade at school, thanks to her treasure trove of recycled books, Felipa's reading was more advanced than others her age. The classroom, with its worn-out

111

benches and chalk-covered blackboards, became a stage where the seeds of knowledge flourished under the light of dedication. Felipa, with her inquisitive mind and bright eyes, immersed herself in her lessons with an insatiable hunger to learn.

However, as the days passed and the seasons turned like a carousel, Felipa realized something unusual about herself. Her senses, particularly her sense of smell, had matured in a way that made her different from other children. She could detect the trace of life in every scent that wafted through the air. She could capture the fragrances of pets that accompanied her peers, the faint traces of home left on children's clothing. She could also recognize the scent of those who had not bathed, like an invisible spectrum that only she could see.

But beyond these superficial discoveries, Felipa found that her olfactory gift was an open door to a world of deeper perception. She could discern the emotional traces hidden in people's scents. She could sense the stress that floated like a subtle cloud in the air, as well as the shadows of depression that darkened the essences of those around her.

One day, driven by her intuition and her desire to help others, Felipa found herself in a situation that would change lives. In the classroom, while her teacher was delivering a lesson and the children were lost in their own thoughts, Felipa noticed a subtle aroma, a nuance that hadn't been there before. With the seriousness of an experienced physician, she pointed her index finger towards her teacher. 'Teacher, you need to see a doctor,' Felipa said, her words echoing in the silence of the room.

The teacher, surprised by the girl's audacity and determination, decided to follow her advice. That afternoon, she visited a clinic and underwent a series of tests. The results brought with them a diagnosis that would have gone unnoticed if not for Felipa's keen observation. Ovarian cancer had been detected in its early stages, allowing treatment to begin on time and giving the teacher a real chance at recovery.

Felipa had found her purpose. She was not only the girl who had been rescued by love and friendship in a place forgotten by many, but also a beacon of insight and care, a voice that whispered in the language of senses and empathy.

Inside the warm abode that Pompeya had patiently and lovingly built in the midst of the dump, an intriguing dynamic began to unfold between Felipa and her exceptional sense of smell. As time flowed like a constant river, the girl's senses became a window to a world beyond the conventional. Each day brought new discoveries, and every scent became a clue in the mystery that was life itself.

Pompeya, with her life experience and maternal intuition, began to suspect that Felipa's ability to detect scents went beyond mere chance. On more than one occasion, as Pompeya was preparing their dinner, Felipa would voice her observations from a considerable distance. 'The soup needs more salt and seasoning.'

Pompeya, initially puzzled, decided to follow the girl's intuition. Taking the spoon in her hands, she tasted the soup with a mixture of curiosity and skepticism. Indeed, the flavors required a dose of salt and seasoning to achieve culinary perfection. Astonishment and admiration filled Pompeya's eyes as she looked at Felipa.

Nor was Felipa's keen perception limited to the kitchen. In the bustling Agua Fría market, where voices and aromas intertwined in a harmonious chaos, Felipa remained a keen observer of her surroundings. One day, as they strolled among the fruit and vegetable stalls, Felipa approached a woman with a friendly smile. 'You have a baby in there,' Felipa said with the certainty of a seer who had glimpsed through the veil of time.

The woman looked at her with momentary bewilderment before continuing on her way. Pompeya, accustomed to Felipa's acuteness, simply watched the exchange with an indulgent smile.

However, time, which is often an ally in the revelation of truth, brought forth a surprising revelation. Several months later, Pompeya crossed paths again with the same woman in the market. The months had left their mark on the woman, whose figure had subtly changed.

Pompeya greeted her warmly, and the woman responded with a shy yet delighted gesture. 'Do you remember when my girl told you that you were expecting a baby?' Pompeya asked, her eyes sparkling with curiosity.

The woman nodded with a smile, and a light of understanding and wonder illuminated her face. 'Yes, I remember. At that moment, I couldn't believe it. But then, a few weeks later, I found out I was pregnant. It was a wonderful surprise,' the woman confessed.

Pompeya nodded with a mixture of astonishment and gratitude. Felipa, with her unique gift, had been the bridge connecting the present and the future, the visible reality and the hidden mystery.

However, not everything in this world of sensations was pleasant for Felipa. The mystery of life, like a painting of lights and shadows, also harbored her fears. Felipa had an intense aversion to mouse nests and snakes lurking in the shadows. On silent nights, her imagination often wove tales of horror in which these creatures turned into mythical monsters lurking in the darkest corners of her world.

Despite her ability to detect scents with almost supernatural precision, Felipa couldn't prevent the feeling of panic from engulfing her when she was near these nests. They were like doors to a world that challenged her courage, a reminder that even the most special gifts could coexist with human weaknesses.

In school, her gift made her an intriguing and sometimes intimidating presence to her peers. Childhood games like hide-and-seek became sources of resentment. Children quickly discovered that playing hide-and-seek with Felipa was an impossible task; her keen senses made her an unbeatable seeker, capable of perceiving subtle changes in her friends' scent as they hid.

The games that had once been sources of laughter and fun became symbols of Felipa's loneliness. But her spirit remained unbroken. She always found ways to have fun and connect with others, whether by exploring the dump with Laika or immersing herself in the worlds offered by discarded books.

Felipa's gift transcended the boundaries of everyday life and often placed her in situations where she could make a difference. Her ability to perceive through smell led her to recognize those deserving of her trust and those who were not. One day, as fate wove the threads of danger and opportunity, Felipa became an unwitting heroine.

On a mild sunny afternoon, while Pompeya attended to her daily tasks, a thief lurked in the shadows of the dump. Stealthily, the thief edged towards Pompeya's unattended purse. But Felipa, with her sharp sense of smell, sensed the stranger's presence. Her intuition sounded like a silent scream in her mind, warning her of the impending danger.

Without hesitation, Felipa sprang into action. With the skill of a hunter pursuing its prey, she crept up behind the thief. The dogs, faithful guardians of the girl and the dump, sensed the tension in the air and hurried to her side. Their fierce barks filled air, and the thief, panicking, knocked over a steep pile of rubbish, revealing his presence.

The combination of Felipa's cunning and the warning of the loyal canines was enough to force the thief to flee in panic. Pompeya's purse remained untouched, and her gratitude toward the girl who had perceived the threat was immense. In that moment, Felipa's gift became an invisible shield that protected those she loved and challenged even the darkest shadows.

As Felipa's story wove itself into the tapestry of time, it continued to unveil the mysteries and wonders of a world that only she could see and feel. The days in the dump carried on their unchanging dance, but Felipa's heart and senses kept discovering new nuances in the canvas of life. Her gift, both a blessing and a burden, manifested with every heartbeat, like a lighthouse illuminating the hidden secrets of her surroundings.

The certainty of her abilities echoed in Pompeya's soul. One afternoon at the market, the hustle and bustle of the crowd were interrupted by the desperate cries of a woman. Tragedy had knocked at her door in the cruelest way possible: her child had been snatched from her arms by unknown hands.

The mother pleaded for help, searching for her child amidst the shadows of the crowded market. Yet the crowd, focused on their own concerns, seemed oblivious to the mother's pain. Vendors continued to offer their goods, customers haggled endlessly, and the frenetic rhythm of life continued its course without mercy.

The police arrived at the scene, but they faced an enigma they didn't know how to solve. No one had seen anything, no one knew anything. The police had no clue where to begin their search. Amidst the confusion and despair, a voice rose above the chaos, a voice that resonated like an echo of clarity in everyone's mind. 'I know where they went!' exclaimed Felipa, her voice firm and determined.

The girl's words acted like a beacon guiding ships to safety in the midst of a storm. The mother, driven by desperation and hope, clung to Felipa like a lifebuoy in a turbulent ocean. She took the girl's arm, her eyes filled with tears, seeking in the child a promise that everything would be okay. With no other option but to follow the girl, the mother, the police, and Pompeya began their journey through a labyrinth of scents and mysteries.

Like a musical score, the path to the truth unfolded before Felipa. She navigated through the crowd, which seemed to close like a river flowing in different directions. Her sense of smell, sharp as a hawk's eye, separated the scents of people and things, like a prism revealing hidden colors in light.

They walked, guided by Felipa's gift, until they reached a seedy hotel on the outskirts of town. Its weathered walls and broken windows bore silent witness to dark secrets. Felipa pointed to a door with a confidence that only her gift could provide.

The police knocked without hesitation, but silence was the only response. Yet their trust in the girl's gifts was absolute. Beneath kicks that resonated like drums of justice, the door yielded to the force of the law and hope. There, in the dark room, were the kidnapper and the child.

The mother, finally free from the grip of fear, clung to her child as if time itself had stopped, her eyes filled with tears of relief and gratitude. The exposed kidnapper eluded justice no longer. The mother's resilience, Felipa's audacity, and the strength of the law had united in a symphony of courage and determination. The story, woven in the corridors of the market and the dark corners of the dump, had found its climax in the liberation of a child and the triumph of truth.

As the sun sank on the horizon, painting the sky with golden and crimson hues, the municipal dump, which had silently witnessed so many stories, continued to guard its secrets and treasures. And in the heart of the landfill and in Felipa's soul, the story continued to be woven, with every scent, every encounter, and every challenge, in a narrative that reminded everyone that even in the darkest places, the light of courage and truth could find its way.

As the years marched on, life in the landfill continued its endless dance, weaving stories of love and loss in the shadows of memories. Felipa and Laika, two souls intertwined by invisible bonds, had become a symbol of companionship and strength in a world where loneliness lurked in every corner. Together, they had faced challenges and discovered the secrets of that peculiar world they inhabited.

But as the whims of destiny often dictate, a day came when Felipa and Laika's paths abruptly and cruelly diverged. It happened in a fleeting instant when the roar of an engine and the screeching of tires unleashed chaos. A car struck Laika, and the world seemed to stop in that moment of horror.

Felipa's heart pounded like a frantic drum as her eyes fixed on the figure of the car receding in the distance. Shock and helplessness engulfed her, and a silent scream echoed within. The world around her darkened, as if tragedy had drained the colors into shadow.

Laika, her loyal companion, lay on the ground, her eyes searching for Felipa. In an instant, the life they had shared became a fragile memory. Tears welled up in Felipa's eyes, a torrent of pain that seemed endless. She knelt beside Laika, caressed her one last time, and whispered words of love and gratitude.

The car had vanished like a ghost, leaving Felipa with a broken heart and a sense of injustice burning in her chest. Time seemed to stand still, a silent echo of love and loss now filling her world.

Grief overcame Felipa like a dark shroud. The air felt heavier, the colors less vibrant, and her heart filled with a void that seemed impossible to fill. Pompeya, a witness to the child's agony, tried to console her, but Felipa sank deeper and deeper into the abyss of sadness. Pompeya, meanwhile, couldn't help but feel a mix of envy and admiration for the bond between Felipa and Laika. While Pompeya wished for Felipa to find solace, she couldn't help but feel on the outside of that unique and powerful relationship.

In her grief and solitude, Felipa found a special place in her heart for Laika. She buried her near her home, in a place where she could visit and bring flowers, as a constant tribute to the loyalty and love they had shared. Days turned into weeks, and weeks into months of silent mourning. Each day, next to Laika's grave, Felipa left a piece of her soul, keeping the flame of her memory alive.

The loss of Laika, her spiritual mother, was a blow that was difficult to overcome. Felipa found herself amidst a sea of conflicting emotions: the sadness that enveloped her like a shadow and the feeling that something had been lost forever. The municipal dump, which had once been a place of shared adventures and discoveries, now seemed like a silent echo of what it had been.

The wound in her heart didn't close easily, but time, that eternal healer, began to dull the sharpest pain. The dump remained her refuge and her home, and Laika, in spirit, remained by her side. The memory of her became a source of strength for Felipa. Pompeya, on the other hand, began to fall prey to the greed that sometimes nests in human hearts.

The desire for material wealth seemed to have taken hold of Pompeya like an insidious shadow. Her eyes gleamed with the promise of riches as she observed Felipa, whose gifts had proven to be far more extraordinary than anyone could have imagined. Greed had become the backdrop of her mind, and her thoughts were woven with the thread of self-interest. 'Where did you get such an extraordinary sense of smell?' Pompeya inquired on one occasion, her words laden with expectation and greed.

Felipa's response, sweet and sincere, resonated in the air like a melody in a fairy tale. 'I don't know. I think it was Laika's milk that gave me this ability,' Felipa said, her voice carrying with it the nostalgia of shared memories.

Felipa's words took Pompeya on a journey through time, to when Laika had been Felipa's protector and provider of food. The memories of those moments, like diamonds buried in the sands of history, shone before them, illuminating the bonds that had united the girl and her faithful friend.

'I also remember when my mother abandoned me at the chapel of Our Lady of the Scavengers. Laika found me and gave me her teat so I could have her milk. Then you came and picked me up from the landfill,' Felipa revealed with a calm that seemed to touch the supernatural.

Pompeya was left speechless by Felipa's narration. The girl's words seemed to have unearthed memories of a time long left behind in the shadows of memory. Felipa's story, woven with threads of abandonment and providence, presented itself to Pompeya as an unexpected revelation.

The girl had been a witness to her own history, like a silent observer in the shadows of the past. Laika's milk, the love of an adoptive mother in the form of a dog, had left an indelible trace in Felipa's very essence. Her mind retained moments that most would have lost in the nebulousness of time.

The silence stretched between them. Pompeya found herself immersed in a mixture of astonishment and fear. How was it possible that Felipa could remember her childhood events so clearly, even when she was so young?

Pompeya, with eyes that seemed to hold a glint of insatiable desire, sought answers in Felipa's words. Curiosity had blended with greed in her pursuit of a benefit that could be gleaned from the girl's unique abilities.

'Do you know who your mother is?' Pompeya asked, her words hanging in the air like a leaf suspended in the breeze.

Felipa's response, laden with profound yet serene sadness, echoed like a whisper in the stillness of the dump. 'I don't know who she is, but I still remember her scent. If I smell her again, I'll know it's her,' Felipa replied, her words carrying with them the nostalgia of a lost bond in the mists of time.

Pompeya, a hint of empathy in her eyes, contemplated the girl before her. The search for identity, an enigma that often proves more challenging than the most intricate puzzles, seemed to be the burden Felipa carried in her heart. The unique fragrance of a mother, imprinted in her deepest memories, had become a beacon of hope amidst the darkness of uncertainty.

But Pompeya's greed had unearthed a question that held much more pragmatic value for her. 'And can you smell illnesses?' she inquired, her words outlining the part of the matter that interested her the most.

Felipa's words, simple and sincere, rang in the air like notes from a forgotten melody. 'Yes, but I don't know the names of most of them.'

Felipa's gift, as wondrous as it was mysterious, allowed her to detect the scent of suffering and illness. Although she lacked the medical language to offer a diagnosis, Felipa's instinct resonated in the fabric of her being, like an intuitive connection to the struggles and challenges faced by those around her.

Seasons came and went, leaving traces on the landscape and in the hearts of those who dwelled within the municipal dump's confines. Felipa, now a twelve-year-old girl, stood at a pivotal point in her life, at a crossroads where knowledge and ethics collided in a whirlwind of decisions.

Pompeya's mind had not rested in its search for opportunities. During the long nights sitting in their humble dwelling, she had devised a plan to leverage Felipa's gift. The greed that had begun to sprout took root in Pompeya's heart like an insidious seed. The girl, Pompeya thought, would become a kind of oracle, capable of identifying diseases by their characteristic scents.

With that purpose in mind, Pompeya took Felipa to a hospital for the terminally ill, a place where the battle against disease and adversity often ended in defeat. It was a place of shadows and suffering, but also of humanity and hope, where lives frequently intersected in search of relief and solace.

'Approach the sick and tell them you're here to pray for them. Then ask them what disease afflicts them. They will answer you because the terminally ill always want to talk about their illness.

Focus on smelling that disease and memorize its name,' instructed Pompeya.

Pompeya's words were like pieces of a puzzle that Felipa attempted to assemble in her mind. The line between knowledge and exploitation seemed to blur amid mixed intentions. Felipa, with her noble soul and genuine desire to help, found herself at a crossroads.

And so, with Pompeya's instructions in her mind and a mix of emotions in her heart, Felipa approached the patients. Like a ray of light amidst the shadows, she offered her prayers and attention to those who so desperately needed a respite on their final journey.

The girl spoke with each patient, her voice gentle and warm, and listened attentively as they shared the burdens of their illnesses. As she listened to their words, Felipa breathed deeply, trying to absorb the aroma that accompanied each disease. Her senses, sharper than ever, began to identify the subtleties in the air, the olfactory notes that set each disease apart.

But as she progressed in her mission, Felipa couldn't help but feel a deeper connection with the terminally ill. Empathy flowed in her heart, weaving invisible threads between her and those who shared their stories. They were not just smells; they were voices of struggle and suffering that resonated in her soul.

Felipa not only learned the names of diseases but also learned to understand human pain more deeply. Instead of a mere diagnostic machine, she was becoming a source of compassion and support for those who had faced adversity with bravery.

Weeks turned into months, and Felipa continued her work in the hospital. Her abilities evolved beyond the identification of odors. Her presence brought comfort and companionship to the patients. And in turn, Felipa felt she had purpose in caring for others.

As the months passed, Felipa became a blessing in the hospital. Her abilities to detect diseases and locate malignant tumors became a source of wonder and admiration.

The girl, with her simplicity and innate wisdom, approached doctors with precise information about the location of malignant tumors. Her words were like small gems of knowledge cast into the uncertainty of medical diagnosis. 'I know where this patient's tumor is. Do you want to operate?' Felipa would say, with the serenity of someone who had deciphered a secret enigma.

The doctors exchanged looks of disbelief. Could it be true that this child, whose home was in the shadows of the dump, possessed knowledge that challenged the boundaries of medical science? Their hearts wrestled between suspicion and curiosity. They would not listen to Pompeya, who, in her desire to profit from Felipa's gift, joined the conversation. It was only when the patient himself spoke up that the doctors took notice. 'Follow the girl's instructions; she is the Virgin of the Dump!' exclaimed the patient with a fervor that echoed through the corridors of the hospital.

The mention of this sacred title, uttered by lips that had known suffering and struggle, changed the course of the conversation. The doctors, moved by the patient's desperation and faith, finally decided to follow Felipa's instructions.

The girl, thus elevated, did not let the title bestowed upon her sway her. Her focus remained on the well-being of those who suffered, those who had known nothing but trials and challenges. She became a voice pointing the way to healing, a guide in a world of uncertainty.

The doctors, guided by the patient's trust and the certainty instilled by Felipa, carried out the operation. What they found in the terminally ill patient's body left everyone speechless: the tumor was exactly where Felipa had indicated. Surprise and admiration filled the operating room, like a silent choir singing the praise of the inexplicable.

Felipa, the Virgin of the Dump, had left an indelible mark on the lives of those who had crossed her path. Her gift transcended not only the sense of smell but also awakened faith and compassion in the hearts of those around her. As the sun rose and set over the dump, Felipa continued to weave a tale that, though it oscillated between the earthly and the transcendental, was imbued with the very essence of humanity in all its complexity and beauty.

***

Days and nights wove their song on the canvas of life, and Felipa remained a beacon of hope in the dark sea of illness and suffering. The legend of the Virgin of the Dump expanded like an echo on the breezes of northern Puebla and Veracruz, carrying with it stories of miraculous healing and a gift that defied the boundaries of logic.

Over time, the hospital for the destitute and terminally ill became a sanctuary of faith and hope, with Felipa as its guardian. Like a loving shadow, she approached each bed with a smile and a word of encouragement. But one day, her steps led her to a bed that held something different. 'Sister, what is your illness so that I may pray for you?' Felipa inquired, her voice like a breeze whispering secrets to the wind.

The lady in the bed, with a serene countenance, responded with gratitude in her gaze: 'Thank you for your kindness, sister, but I am not sick; I am resting in this bed. I am a volunteer; I am here to help.'

The truth resonated in her words, but Felipa, like a leaf swaying in the breeze, carried certainty in her senses. A subtle scent, a fraction of a second in which aromas intertwined with understanding, revealed the absence of illness in the lady's body. An understanding that transcended the physical, rooted in intuition and connection. 'Sister, how do you manage to stay so healthy?' Felipa inquired, her eyes shining with undeniable fascination.

The lady shared her secrets with humility and wisdom, revealing the habits and choices that had forged her health. Each piece of advice, each conscious choice, resonated with the truth of a life in balance with nature. It was then that the pieces of the puzzle in Felipa's mind began to fit together into a complete picture. The lady's words were like seeds falling into her mind and sprouting into a revelation as clear as spring water, and Felipa realized that diseases were often the result of choices and habits that deviated from natural harmony.

From that moment on, Felipa's purpose took on a new dimension. Her vision transcended the healing of individual illnesses to embrace a larger cause: the promotion of health in its most elemental form. The power of the dump, with its hidden treasures and secrets to discover, manifested itself in the form of a girl carrying a message of change and transformation.

Felipa, with the authority of her experience and the passion of her heart, began to share her discoveries with the patients of the hospital. A vegetarian diet, the rejection of processed foods, and the promotion of a life in harmony with nature became her message. And her influence, like a rising tide, changed the course of the hospital.

The hospital's leadership embraced her message. Processed drinks and foods were banished, and the diet transformed into a reflection of the wisdom she had learned. The sanctuary that had once been the last stop on life's journey became a beacon of health and transformation, a community that embraced nature and rejected the paths of illness. The Virgin of the Dump, with her unique gift and passionate heart, had brought a light that guided the community towards a new path in the pursuit of health and happiness.

***

Life unfolded like a rich and complex narrative, woven with threads of fame, kindness, and envy. Felipa, the Virgin of the Dump, had transcended the boundaries of her home in the dump to become a beacon of hope. Her gift, like a rare and unique jewel, shone in the darkness of human suffering, offering a glimpse of light amidst uncertainty. The needy came to her with the confidence that her prodigious sense of smell would provide relief and hope. Every day, the hospice bore witness to her tireless dedication to the well-being of others.

However, in the shadows cast by Felipa's light, Pompeya's envy grew ever greater. Greed had dug its claws into her heart, dimming her appreciation for Felipa's nobility and love. While the community praised the Virgin of the Dump, Pompeya coveted the imagined riches that could come from her abilities.

The contrast between Felipa's kindness and Pompeya's selfish interests reflected the eternal battle between light and darkness. While Felipa extended her hands to offer healing and hope, Pompeya saw financial opportunities in every diagnosis the girl provided. Envy and greed threatened to consume what had once been a relationship of care and love.

One morning, Pompeya, with a glint in her eyes that barely concealed her intent, woke Felipa early. The girl, still in the folds of sleep, peered out the window and was left breathless by the sight. A crowd had gathered outside her home. Anxious gazes, faces marked by suffering and uncertainty, sought relief from their sorrows. Eyes that had shed tears of despair now fixed on her, as if her presence were the key to dispelling the pain that lay in their hearts.

Among the crowd, a young man pushed his way forward urgently, his desperate eyes searching for the gaze of the Virgin of the Dump. With a moan, he exclaimed: 'My heart is racing; I think I'm going to have a heart attack!'

Felipa observed the drama unfolding before her, but a spark of understanding and humor shone in her eyes. Gently, like someone unraveling an enigma, she asked: 'Have you felt like this before, on other occasions?' The young man nodded vigorously, his hands clutching his chest, as if he could calm the racing of his heart with his touch.

Felipa couldn't help but burst into laughter, a laughter that echoed like a beacon of light amidst the tension. People looked on, bewildered by the girl's reaction, but Felipa's laughter was like a refreshing breeze that dispelled the heaviness in the air. 'Forgive me for laughing,' Felipa said, regaining her composure, 'but your problem isn't a heart attack. Your problem is panic attacks.'

Her words flowed from her lips with the tranquility of someone who had found the key to deciphering an enigma. With patience and tenderness, she explained to the young man what panic attacks were, how they manifested, and how he could prevent them. Every word she uttered was a flash of wisdom, a drop of relief in the ocean of his anguish.

The young man, amazed and relieved, listened attentively. His eyes, once clouded by anxiety, now lit up with understanding and hope. Embracing Felipa's words like a precious gift, he walked away with a lighter step and a less burdened heart.

The crowd continued to wait, eager, but now there was a glint of curiosity and anticipation in their eyes. Felipa's laughter and her ability to unravel suffering with words of wisdom had captured their attention. That day, in the midst of the crowd gathered at her feet, Felipa once again demonstrated that her gift resided not only in her prodigious sense of smell but also in the compassion and understanding that radiated from her heart.

And so, on that day of encounters and revelations, the Virgin of the Dump left her mark on the souls of those who had come in search of relief. With each shared smile, with each word of comfort, a deeper connection was forged between Felipa and her community. The thread of hope was woven with each interaction, reminding them that, in the midst of darkness, there was always a guiding light toward healing and well-being.

That day, the skies seemed woven with threads of nostalgia and longing. Felipa ventured into the streets of Agua Fría with expectation pulsing in her chest. The wind played with the folds of her hair as her steps resonated on the pavement, like the chords of a song whose lyrics she had not yet discovered.

The trace of a scent reached her nose, a fragrance that whispered of the past, of moments lying in the depths of her memory like hidden gems. It was the scent she had been searching for since she could remember: the aroma of her biological mother. Although she had been just a baby when she was abandoned in the chapel of Our Lady of the Scavengers, that scent had become ingrained in her being, an indelible mark of the maternal connection that had been severed before it could flourish.

Felipa followed the trail with her heart beating strongly in her chest. Each step brought her closer to the possibility of finding the source of that scent that had been her silent companion for so many years. The path led her to the market, where scents intertwined in a vibrant mosaic. However, right at the entrance of the market, the trail vanished like a dream upon waking.

Frustration welled up in her chest like a tide, threatening to wash away her hopes and longings. Desperately, she tried to rediscover that elusive trail, exploring every nook and cranny, like a detective following the clues of an intriguing mystery. But the fragrance had dissipated, like a sigh lost in the wind.

Perhaps her mother had climbed into a car and driven away, like a shooting star fading into the vastness of the night sky. Felipa found herself standing in the middle of the market, her heart filled with a tumult of emotions. Hope had been fleeting, but it had left a mark on her heart, a spark of possibilities that continued to burn within her.

That night, as the sky was painted with the warm hues of sunset, Felipa stood in front of the chapel of Our Lady of the Scavengers, gazing at the unchanging figure that had been a silent witness to her life. The breeze caressed her skin, carrying with it the echo of her desires. The spark of hope still burned within her, reminding her that every path, even if it seemed to disappear into the distance, led to its destination eventually.

And so, as the stars began to dot the sky and the moon rose majestically on its silver throne, Felipa looked up at the firmament, as if she could find in the stars an answer to the mysteries of her past and the destinies intertwined in her present. In the heart of the night, the girl with the prodigious sense of smell became a symbol of the eternal quest for love and connection, a quest that would lead her down unknown paths and mysteries yet to be discovered.

***

The days passed like the pages of a book slipping through the curious fingers of an eager reader. Felipa, imbued with determination and hope, continued her work at the dump while her heart beat to the rhythm of her deepest desires. Every time the wind played with the scents mingling in the air, her senses rose like antennae, ready to capture the essence she so yearned for.

On a golden afternoon, Felipa wandered through the dump, collecting forgotten items and rescuing treasures from the tangle of waste. A gentle breeze caressed her skin, and her nostrils caught a fragrance that made her stop in her tracks. It was her once again: the essence she had been searching for. She followed the scent to a corner of the landfill that seemed neglected even by the forsaken objects that lay there.

Her heart pounding, Felipa followed the trail. The scent grew more intense, each step bringing her closer to the meeting she had yearned for. She imagined what that moment would be like, how she would embrace her, how she would tell her about her life, the things she had learned, the mysteries she had unraveled, and the lives she had touched.

But, like in a cosmic dance, the scent trail faded once again. Felipa stood in the middle of the dump, her eyes closed, trying to hold onto the fragrance in her mind, as if she could recreate it through the power of her will. However, the wind had taken its capricious course and had carried away the trail she so desired.

Twilight spilled over the horizon. Felipa remained unmoving, enveloped in a silence that resonated with the melody of her thoughts. Despite the disappointment, she knew she wouldn't give up. Every fleeting encounter with the trail of her biological mother brought her closer. She could feel it in the air, like the changing of seasons heralding the arrival of spring.

And so, with the night spreading its blanket of stars overhead, Felipa continued her journey, knowing that each day brought new opportunities and that destiny continued to weave her story with threads of mystery and hope.

***

The reputation of the Virgin of the Dump grew with every life Felipa touched, every accurate diagnosis she provided, and every heart that healed thanks to her unique abilities. Patients came from all over, seeking answers and solutions in Felipa's clear eyes. In squares and marketplaces, in parks and makeshift hospitals, she listened to the stories of the afflicted with patience and empathy. Like a modern oracle, she pointed with her finger to the exact location of the ailment, illuminating the path to healing.

But while Felipa received gratitude and admiration, Pompeya continued to be consumed by resentment that grew like a dark shadow in her heart. She couldn't understand why Felipa refused to accept money for her services, even though they could have left behind the poverty that surrounded them. For Pompeya, life in the landfill became increasingly bitter as she watched the crowds flock to her protege in search of answers.

The relationship between Pompeya and Felipa became tense. Silences became uncomfortable, words that once flowed like a river became scarce and laden with frustration. Every time Felipa rejected an offer of money, Pompeya felt that her sacrifice and support were not adequately valued. But despite it all, Felipa continued her work, tending to the sick regardless of their social status or ability to pay. The girl from the landfill had become a symbol of kindness, compassion, and healing power. Although their relationship was at a crossroads, Pompeya could not ignore the wonder she had helped to create, nor the reality that Felipa was bringing light and relief to those who needed it most.

Yet with each passing day, Felipa's emotional burden grew heavier. The responsibility of facing the tragedies of others, of revealing heartbreaking diagnoses, and of carrying the hopes of those desperately seeking a cure, began to take its toll on her sensitive spirit. Despite pleas and offers of money, Felipa couldn't perform miracles. Her ability to smell illness and emotions was not a cure for all the world's ailments. Every time she faced a case without a solution, she felt the weight of her impotence, the burden of bearing witness to the fragility of human life.

In her small refuge in the landfill, Felipa cried silently for those she couldn't help. As her abilities became more in demand, her time was divided between moments of triumph and moments of lament. Although she had saved many, she always felt the weight of those who had remained beyond her reach.

In those moments of vulnerability, Pompeya tried to be a support for Felipa, understanding the emotional burden she carried. Despite their differences and resentments, Pompeya had witnessed the nobility of Felipa's heart. The woman from the landfill admired the girl's strength, who carried the weight of others' tragedies on her shoulders.

One day, a wealthy man brought his young son, who was suffering from leukemia, and begged Felipa to save him. Desperate, the man offered her money. Felipa covered her face with her hands and began to cry, telling the man: 'I'm so sorry, sir, there is no cure for your son's illness.'

Felipa's tears resonated in the heart of the wealthy man, who looked at the girl with tears in his eyes. Although desperate to save his son's life, he also understood the sadness that Felipa carried, and was grateful for her candor. He thanked the girl for her honesty and left with his son in his arms, leaving behind the scent of hopelessness and resignation.

Pompeya watched Felipa's refusal of the man's money with growing fury. Every attempt she had made to convince Felipa to take payment for her work had failed, and now Pompeya's thoughts took a darker turn. In private, she schemed up plans to discredit Felipa. She couldn't bear to be overshadowed by the young prodigy, whose achievements and virtues placed her on a pedestal that Pompeya longed to reach. Every time praise and gratitude were directed at Felipa, a sting of bitterness pierced Pompeya's heart.

Her twisted thoughts led her to devise ways to trip Felipa up, to cast doubt on her ability and authenticity. However, she didn't dare to openly act against her, fearing that the community would shun her for attacking the beloved and respected figure of the Virgin of the Dump.

Meanwhile, Felipa continued with her work, unaware of the storm brewing around her. Her days were filled with consultations, diagnoses, and advice that alleviated the suffering of the sick. And as the sick and dying came and went, nor could she forget the quest for her own identity. The trail of her biological mother's scent continued to appear at unexpected moments, reminding her that her personal history remained an unresolved mystery. Each time the trail appeared to her, her heart beat with the hope of a reunion, but also with the fear of what she might discover.

The town, meanwhile, couldn't help but notice the increasing tension between Felipa and Pompeya. Rumors mingled with reality, creating an atmosphere charged with intrigue and mixed emotions. Some suspected Pompeya's envy and greed, while others preferred to ignore the signs of discord and continue seeking the guidance and relief that only Felipa could provide.

Indeed, Felipa's fame had grown so great that there were calls for her to travel beyond Agua Fría to reach those unable to make the journey to the dump. And so, much to Pompeya's annoyance, Felipa agreed to embark on a pilgrimage.

During her journey, she visited many municipalities in Mexico until she reached the outskirts of Tenochtitlán. However, the city's oligarchs prevented her from entering, fearing Felipa's positive influence on the Mexicas people. Therefore, Felipa decided to carry out a healing service outside the great city; she needed a spacious place to gather thousands of worshippers. She found a large plot of vacant land near Lake Texcoco where she could hold such an event.

No one knew exactly how many people attended, but news helicopters reported nearly half a million people present. There were seas of people for several kilometers around. All the news channels were there to witness this historic moment in Mexico. The Virgin of the Dump captured the attention of the entire country. Before going out to give her speech, Felipa took a moment to take in the sea of people who had come from

Tenochtitlán. She felt unbearable nerves; her hands were sweating. She couldn't understand how it was possible that so many people were there to see an eighteen-year-old.

The cool breeze blowing of Lake Texcoco gently caressed her face, and Felipa stood on the improvised stage, looking out at the crowd. The view was overwhelming: an ocean of anxious and hopeful faces that had come to hear her words and be touched by her presence. Although young in age, the wisdom radiating from her eyes was undeniable.

The sun began to set as the murmur of the crowd filled the air. Hundreds of thousands of people from different parts of the country had left behind their daily worries and burdens to be part of this historic moment. The hope for change shone in their eyes.

The noise of cameras and media microphones created a constant buzz in the background. When Felipa stepped out to speak at the microphone, there was a roar and applause from the people. However, before she began to speak, the Virgin of the Dump felt a change in atmospheric pressure, something was amiss. Confused for a few seconds, she didn't understand why birds were fleeing Tenochtitlán. Felipa interpreted what was happening and shouted with all her might: 'Earthquake! Everyone, outside! An earthquake is coming!' People were confused, both at the pilgrimage and those watching on the television in their homes. 'Get out of wherever you are! An earthquake is coming!'

People screamed and ran out of their homes. Others hesitated, as the earthquake alarm had not yet sounded. When it finally did, the earthquake itself started just seconds later, though several minutes had gone by since Felipa's warning.

Fortunately, many people managed to get outside in time. Chaos reigned for minutes that felt like hours as people screamed and cried in anguish, feeling the earth shake. Panic and desperation spread from Tenochtitlán to southern Oaxaca.

The earth continued to shake fiercely, as if Mother Nature had awakened in anger. Buildings creaked and swayed; some collapsed into clouds of dust and rubble, while others tenaciously withstood the onslaught. Amid the chaos, the crowd that had attended Felipa's pilgrimage struggled to keep their balance, clutching whatever they could as the ground continued to tremble beneath their feet.

Felipa herself fought to stay on her feet; her hands held tightly to the podium as her heart beat intensely. The warning she had given had been crucial, but now her attention was divided between staying calm and ensuring that everyone present could escape unharmed.

The crowd began to move amid the confusion, seeking a safe place away from the buildings that could collapse. Some tried to call their loved ones, while others sought refuge in the open spaces of the land. Despite the fear and chaos, many could be seen helping each other, offering a helping hand and words of encouragement. Adversity had united the crowd in an attempt to overcome the danger they faced. All the while, the earth continued its deafening rumble.

After minutes that seemed like an eternity, the earthquake finally began to decrease in intensity. The earth stopped shaking with the same ferocity, and the crowd began to regain calm slowly. Hearts continued to beat rapidly, but the worst of the danger had passed.

The afternoon was illuminated by emergency lights and flashlights as rescuers and volunteers began to work in the search for people trapped and injured. Despite the destruction and pain, solidarity became evident, and the will to help and rebuild filled the atmosphere.

Felipa, amid tears and hugs of gratitude, felt profound relief seeing that her warning had saved many lives. Although her words had been incomprehensible at first, her intuition had been correct. She was overwhelmed by the magnitude of the event and the people's response to the tragedy.

The Virgin of the Dump spoke into the microphone and said, 'We must rescue our brothers and sisters trapped under the rubble!' She went from building to building, indicating to people the exact location of those trapped. She went three days without sleep, food, or rest until she finally collapsed from exhaustion. When she woke up two days later, she received the news that more than three hundred people had been rescued thanks to her sense of smell, which allowed authorities to locate those trapped.

Days and weeks passed, and Tenochtitlán began to recover from the tragedy. People thanked Felipa for rescuing so many. She gained the love of the Mexica people, who idolized and admired her with great reverence. Even the city's oligarchs allowed Felipa to make her triumphant entrance into Tenochtitlán. She reached the Zócalo, which was filled with people cheering for her, throwing flowers as she walked by, and chanting her name. The young prodigy, the Virgin of the Dump, moved through the crowd with a mixture of humility and gratitude in her heart. She had lived through so many experiences, from her birth in the landfill to this moment of triumph and recognition. The intensity of emotions overwhelmed her as she advanced toward the stage that had been prepared for her.

Pompeya, observing from a distance, felt a mix of envy, resentment, and fury. She could no longer bear the admiration and love the people felt for Felipa. As she watched the crowd acclaiming the young girl, a twisted idea began to form in her mind. An idea that would represent her final attempt to displace Felipa and seize her abilities.

After the earthquake, Felipa returned to Agua Fría to rest for a few days and recover before continuing her pilgrimages. Pompeya no longer concealed her hatred for her, and the dense energies she emanated made Felipa uncomfortable. This prompted her to plan a new pilgrimage as soon as possible. However, something happened that delayed her plans: Felipa once again encountered the essence of her biological mother in the streets of Agua Fría.

Felipa, with her heart filled with mixed emotions, set out to follow the trail of her biological mother's essence once again. She would explore every corner of Agua Fría for even the slightest trace of her scent. The urgency to know the woman who had given her life became an insatiable passion.

Every day, Felipa walked the streets, squares, and corners of the city, following the trail that faded and reappeared. Every time she caught the scent, she filled with hope and excitement, only to watch it disappear once more.

As the days went by, Felipa began to receive curious glances from the residents of Agua Fría. Her intense pursuit did not go unnoticed. Some admired her tenacity, while others viewed her with skepticism and mocked her efforts. Despite the rumors and curious looks from the locals, Felipa did not stop. Nights of insomnia and relentless days followed. She longed for that long-awaited encounter that would finally allow her to meet the woman who had given her life.

One morning, there was a knock on Felipa's door. She was informed that a man needed her help to find his daughter. Felipa quickly prepared herself and accompanied the man. They arrived at his house, and the man explained the situation. 'Last night, around eleven, I was here drinking beer with my best friend, but after that, I don't remember anything. This morning, Nana María came and woke me up to tell me that my daughter wasn't in her bed. I don't understand what happened to her,' the man explained as he knelt and pleaded with Felipa. 'Please, Virgin of the Dump, help me find her, I beg you!'

'What do you call yourself, brother?' Felipa asked.

'José Torres,' the man replied.

'What's your friend's name?' inquired the Virgin.

'Benjamín González,' José said.

Felipa smelled the empty beer bottles on the table and detected the scent of tranquilizers and other drugs. She then headed to José Torres' daughter's bedroom, where she sniffed the scent of a man on the bed. Felipa committed the scent of the man to memory with the purpose of finding the culprit.

With the olfactory essence of both the man and José Torres' daughter imprinted in her memory, Felipa left the house and came to an abrupt halt, closing her eyes as she concentrated her mind on following the trail. The wind blew gently, carrying the various scents of the city. However, among all those aromas, Felipa detected the essence she was looking for, a particular scent that stood out among the rest—the essence of José Torres' daughter.

Guided by her prodigious sense of smell, she began to walk the streets of Agua Fría, with José Torres and a curious crowd following, tracking the subtle clues the scent provided. She ventured into streets and turned corners, feeling the urgency of finding José Torres' daughter. As she advanced, the images of the city blurred around her, and only the scent trail indicated where she must go.

The Virgin of the Dump began to breathe rhythmically. Her senses sharpened, and she could perceive the subtlety of the aromas emanating from the girl's trail. She closed her eyes, and her thoughts became an echo in her mind: 'Focus, feel, connect.' Felipa's heart beat strongly as she observed José Torres' anguish. She knew that time was crucial in situations like these. José Torres looked on with hope as the Virgin of the Dump concentrated her energies on this desperate attempt to bring back his daughter.

The scent led them towards the Tepetate River. They reached the riverbank, and the Virgin of the Dump came to a stop at the water's edge. Her expression changed as she saw the girl's body tangled in tree roots deep in the river's slow-flowing water. She covered her mouth with her hands, and tears welled up in her eyes.

From the other side of the stream, José Torres asked, 'What do you see?' repeating the question with a trembling voice.

The Virgin of the Dump pointed with her hand, an urgent expression on her face. Her eyes, filled with compassion, met those of the desperate father. Without hesitation, José plunged into the murky waters of the Tepetate River. His lungs burned as he descended into the depths, driven by the force of his love and the hope of rescuing his little girl. The water seemed like a separate world, a place where time slowed down, and bubbles danced in a silent ballet.

Finally, his fingers touched something soft and cold on the riverbed. With a surge of renewed energy, he grasped what appeared to be a piece of clothing and, in a desperate movement, resurfaced, holding the lifeless body of his daughter in his arms. His eyes were filled with tears, and his lips murmured prayers and pleas.

As he emerged from the water, he knelt on the shore, tenderly cradling his daughter's fragile body. His hands trembled as he stroked her soaked hair and pale cheeks. José repeated her name over and over, in a desperate attempt to bring her back to life.

The Virgin of the Dump approached with soft steps and knelt beside them. She placed her hand on José's shoulder, offering silent support and a connection that transcended words as José's cries blended with his sobs of grief.

The Virgin of the Dump looked across the river, and her eyes met a shadowy figure rising on the horizon. A jet-black horse advanced with slow and solemn steps, bearing Death herself dressed in black charro attire. In her lap lay José Torres' daughter, her pale and delicate silhouette contrasting with the blackness of the steed.

The girl turned towards her father, her face illuminated by an ethereal glow, and extended a hand in a farewell gesture. Though her lips didn't move, her eyes spoke for her, conveying a message of love and reassurance to José. It was a farewell that transcended words and clung to the heart.

In that moment, the Virgin of the Dump understood that this young girl shared her name, an invisible bond that connected them amidst such disparate circumstances. In the heart of each Felipa beat a unique story woven by the circumstances of their lives and the choices they had made. And though their paths were different, they shared a common thread of compassion and love for those in need.

Benjamín González, José Torres' friend, arrived at the river with a worried and anxious expression. He had heard about the girl's disappearance and wanted to offer his support. However, tension filled the air when the Virgin of the Dump fixed her gaze on him. The words she spoke resonated like thunder in the air. 'Murderer! You're the one responsible!' The accusation from the Virgin of the Dump hit Benjamín González like a direct blow to the heart. He felt stunned and bewildered by the sudden avalanche of words and emotions overwhelming him.

'It was you! It was you! You killed her, murderer!' The Virgin of the Dump shouted desperately. He sought desperately to deny any involvement in what had happened. But his attempt to maintain a façade of innocence was in vain; the powerful gaze of the Virgin seemed to have penetrated his soul and revealed the hidden truth.

In an instant, the scene turned chaotic. The Virgin of the Dump, filled with anger that seemed to have been building up for a long time, lunged at Benjamín González with unleashed fury. Her nails scratched his face, and her hands pulled at his hair. The crowd that had gathered around watched in astonishment, unable to fully understand what was happening. The Virgin of the Dump became an unstoppable force of justice and vengeance, and the crowd was stirred by the display. It didn't take long for collective indignation to turn into a visceral reaction against Benjamín González.

The police finally arrived at the scene, but it was too late to prevent the escalation of violence. The town had taken justice into its own hands. Popular justice had been merciless in its execution, and José Torres' friend paid the price for his dark deed. Silence overtook the place, broken only by the whispers and murmurs of those who witnessed the tragic scene.

The Virgin of the Dump stood there, her gaze fixed on Benjamin Gonzalez's lifeless body. She had channeled the anger and pain of a community that had suffered an unimaginable loss. Although justice had been administered, the price paid was high, and the question of whether there was another way to resolve the situation hung in the air.

***

The death of the young girl, and the terrible justice meted out to her attacker, had taken its toll on Felipa. Agua Fría no longer felt like the safe haven it once had been. And worse, the scent of her birth mother had completely disappeared. Weeks passed with no trace of her. Anxious to escape the disturbed atmosphere of the town, and to fill her days with distraction, the Virgin of the Dump embarked on a new pilgrimage.

Her journey along the Mexico-United States border became an epic event. The pilgrimage attracted hundreds of thousands of people, both from Mexico and the United States. As she traveled through cities and towns along the border, crowds gathered to witness her and receive her blessing. Some traveled long distances just for the chance to be near someone who had demonstrated an extraordinary ability to heal and help.

Reynosa, with its hustle and vibrant culture, welcomed Felipa with open arms. The city turned into a sea of colors and sounds as the crowd followed the Virgin of the Dump on her journey. In Nuevo Laredo, stories of her miracles and charity had preceded her arrival, and people congregated in squares and streets, seeking comfort and hope in her words.

As she crossed the border and reached Ciudad Juárez, the atmosphere became charged with emotion and reverence. The city's residents, who had faced so many challenges and adversities, saw in the Virgin of the Dump a glimmer of hope amidst the darkness. Her words resonated in the hearts of those who had struggled to find a better life on both sides of the border.

Finally, Tijuana became the stage for a touching and profound event. Thousands of people gathered on the beach, gazing out at the ocean as the Virgin of the Dump spoke words of compassion and unity. Her words were directed not only to those present but also to those on the other side of the waters, seeking a better future. In that moment, Felipa seemed to transcend divisions and borders, reminding everyone that humanity shared a common destiny.

As the days and weeks passed, the pilgrimage of the Virgin of the Dump left an indelible mark on the cities along the border. People found solace in her words and hope in her gestures of love and compassion. Her presence served as a reminder that, regardless of circumstances or distances, the power of kindness and empathy had the ability to unite people and transform lives.

Felipa emphasized the lack of proper nutrition as the cause of many diseases, and her goal was to convince people to change their eating habits. 'We must change our eating habits to eradicate the diseases that are causing us so much harm,' Felipa would say to the people. 'We must eat in moderation. Gluttony is robbing us of years of life!' The crowd listened and applauded. 'Diseases are preventable. They are related to our poor eating habits. It's time for a change! It's time to wake up and live a healthy life!'

For Felipa, the mental and physical health of humans was essential to building a better world. But saying it was one thing; achieving it was another.

Felipa knew that to achieve real change in people's eating habits, she had to go beyond words and take concrete actions. She organized workshops and talks in the squares and streets of the cities she visited, sharing practical tips on how to maintain a healthy diet. She invited nutrition and medical experts to join her in educating the community about the benefits of a balanced diet and how they could prevent diseases.

Over time, her efforts bore fruit. People began to pay attention to what they ate, became more conscious of the quality of the food they consumed, and sought healthier options. In local markets, fresh fruits and vegetables became more popular than processed and high-fat foods. Restaurants also adapted by offering healthier menus and vegetarian options.

In addition to her focus on nutrition, Felipa also addressed the importance of mental health. She recognized that mental health was crucial to people's overall well-being and their ability to lead fulfilling lives. She organized workshops on emotional well-being and provided psychological support for those struggling with anxiety, depression, and stress.

As her message spread and her influence grew, government authorities and health organizations began to take notice. Nutrition and health education programs were established in schools and communities. Felipa became a symbol of hope and change, a figure who inspired people to take care of themselves and others.

However, not everyone welcomed her message with open arms. There were those who resisted change, clinging to their old habits and beliefs. Felipa faced criticism and opposition from those who saw her efforts as a threat to their personal or commercial interests. But the strength of her conviction and the love the community had for her propelled her forward, facing challenges with courage and determination.

The legacy of Felipa, the Virgin of the Dump, continued long after her pilgrimage along the border. Her influence left an indelible mark on how people approached their health and well-being. Her teachings transcended geographical and cultural barriers, inspiring people from all walks of life to lead healthier and more fulfilling lives. Her story endured in future generations, reminding them that the power of compassion and dedication could change lives and entire communities.

Finally, the Virgin of the Dump directed her pilgrimage towards southern Mexico, near the border with Guatemala and Belize, tending to the poor, needy, and immigrants arriving in Mexico from the south. There was so much need that Felipa felt overwhelmed by the large number of people seeking a better future. There was so much to do that it seemed like an impossible mission.

In her journey southward, the Virgin of the Dump encountered heart-wrenching stories and desperate situations that moved her to her core. In small towns and communities, she met entire families who had fled violence and poverty in their home countries, seeking refuge and an opportunity to start anew in Mexico.

Felipa tirelessly dedicated herself to providing aid, comfort, and hope to these vulnerable migrants. She organized shelter camps, where food, water, and shelter were provided to newcomers. Alongside local volunteers and humanitarian organizations, she worked tirelessly to offer medical services and legal assistance to those who had crossed the border in search of a better life.

The Virgin of the Dump listened to the stories of those who had left their homes and loved ones behind, facing dangers and hardships on the road to an uncertain future. She offered words of encouragement and compassion, reminding them that they were not alone in their struggle and that there were people willing to help.

Her work did not go unnoticed. Local communities rallied in support of her cause, donating resources and time to alleviate the suffering of migrants. Together, they built temporary shelters, provided education for children, and established training programs for adults, equipping them with tools to rebuild their lives in a new country.

However, they faced significant challenges. The Virgin of the Dump fought against the discrimination and prejudice that migrants sometimes encountered on their journey to a better life. She tirelessly worked to raise awareness about the importance of empathy and solidarity, seeking to change attitudes and build bridges of understanding between local communities and newcomers.

As time passed, Felipa's work began to have a lasting impact on the region. The success stories of migrants who had been supported by her initiative became an inspiration for others. A social change movement emerged, where humanitarian aid and acceptance of immigrants became core values.

The Virgin of the Dump became a symbol of solidarity and hope, a figure that united people beyond borders and cultures. Her pilgrimage through southern Mexico left a lasting legacy of compassion and change, a reminder that even in the most challenging times, the power of humanity could prevail and positively transform lives.

Felipa made the decision to permanently settle in San Cristóbal de las Casas to be close to those in need. She had journeyed so far that her desire to find her mother was now only a dim ache in her heart, not the all-consuming passion it had once been. Now, her heart was with those who required her assistance. Her work in San Cristóbal de las Casas would be her greatest project to date; she envisioned spending the rest of her life in southern Mexico. She was determined; her new life began there.

And so the picturesque San Cristóbal de las Casas became Felipa's new home. The mountains and cobblestone streets resonated with the determined steps of the Virgin of the Dump. Her commitment to the needy knew no bounds, and each day began early with organizing activities to improve the lives of those she served.

The old village chapel was transformed into a refuge of hope. Felipa collaborated with the community to restore and adapt the space, turning it into a comprehensive assistance center for the needy. There, they offered basic education classes, job training workshops, and medical care for those who lacked access to health services.

The fame of the Virgin of the Dump had reached southern Mexico, and people came from all over seeking her guidance and advice. Felipa became a trusted counselor, listening to the stories of pain and struggle of those who had left their homes in search of a better future. With wise words and a compassionate heart, she encouraged each individual to face challenges with courage and perseverance.

Felipa's work also extended to the children and youth of the community. She organized education and recreational programs so they could enjoy a childhood filled with dignity and opportunities. Every smile and every achievement were testaments to the transformative power of her dedication.

Yet still, as she lay awake late at night, her heart still beat with the desire to find her mother, to find answers. Often, she would lose herself in thoughts while walking through the nearby mountains, contemplating the horizon and wondering if someday she would uncover the story behind her abandonment in the landfill.

And in Agua Fría, the shadows of despair and instability loomed ever larger over Pompeya, weaving a dark tapestry of torment in her mind. Her days became a blur of confused moments, incoherent whispers, and vacant stares into the abyss of her own anguish. Reality and fantasy intertwined in a disturbing dance, and her face reflected the inner struggle consuming her.

Isolated in her own world of misery, Pompeya seemed trapped in a labyrinth of tormenting thoughts. Each day, her mind became entangled further in a web of obsessive and fragmented ideas, fueled by her denial of the responsibility she had in her own troubles. Sometimes, her lips moved as if trying to speak to an invisible presence, and her vacant gaze fixated on empty corners, as if searching for answers slipping away.

The anger that had once simmered subtly within her now manifested as an uncontrollable force. Explosions of rage consumed her, and her voice echoed with shouts and curses that cut through the air. The walls of her home bore silent witness to her torment, marked by scratches and broken objects that had succumbed to her unleashed fury. With each passing day, Pompeya sank deeper into the abyss of her own making: madness. Toxic individuals around her, exploiting her vulnerability, fed her paranoia and bitterness, drawing her even closer to the precipice. Her words became more twisted, her laughter more strident, and her gaze more piercing, as if her dark thoughts had materialized in her very appearance.

And so, fate charted its course toward a point of no return. One day, while facing her inner demons in a dark room, Pompeya made the decision that had been haunting her disturbed mind. Armed with her twisted thirst for fame and her tangled perception of reality, she carried out the plan she believed would solve her problems once and for all. She gathered up her belongings and made the long journey from Agua Fría to San Cristóbal de las Casas.

***

The air in the room was charged with unbearable tension as Pompeya and Felipa stood face to face, the past and the present converging in this momentous encounter. The Virgin of the Dump, a symbol of hope and love, could never have imagined that the woman she once called her adoptive mother would become her most ruthless enemy.

Pompeya had arrived with her heart filled with resentment and her mind clouded by obsession. In her eyes burned a dark flame, fueled by years of envy and disdain. The initial embrace was a prelude to the impending storm, for the bitterness that had taken root in Pompeya's soul had finally culminated in an act of violence that would overshadow any other wickedness she had committed.

When Pompeya lunged at Felipa with a knife in hand, the world seemed to pause for a moment. The sharp sound of the blade slicing through the air mingled with Felipa's scream, a cry that resonated with betrayal. The desperate struggle that ensued was like a duel of opposing forces: revenge and love, darkness and light, malice and kindness.

Pompeya's stabs pierced Felipa's body. Each wound was an affront to the purity and compassion that Felipa had radiated throughout her life. Pompeya's face reflected the twisted desire to erase every trace of light in her life, destroying the very image of the Virgin of the Dump.

However, even in the midst of horror and suffering, Felipa found the strength to defend herself. With each blow from her attacker, her determination grew. She fought not only for her own life but also to preserve the hope and kindness she had sown in the hearts of so many in need.

Finally, the storm of violence concluded. Pompeya, exhausted, dropped the knife. Felipa's gaze, still filled with pain, remained a source of love and compassion. Although wounded and weakened, she was not willing to let Pompeya's darkness defeat her.

The steps of tragedy had been marked by hatred and despair, but the story still had room for redemption and forgiveness. The lingering question was whether light could prevail over shadows, whether love could conquer hatred, and whether hope could flourish even in the deepest darkness.

The shadows of tragedy enveloped the scene as the people who had guarded the Virgin of the Dump approached cautiously. Time seemed to have stopped, as if the universe itself were holding its breath in anticipation of an inevitable outcome. The astonished eyes of the witnesses focused on Pompeya, whose body and mind were trapped in a spiral of madness and blood.

Pompeya's body was covered in a macabre dance of crimson, as if the violence she had inflicted on Felipa had left an indelible mark on her being. Her face, once a reflection of jealousy and resentment, now seemed distorted by rage and despair, transforming into a mask of unbridled madness.

Meanwhile, Felipa and Laika reached for one another in a celestial embrace. In that final moment, the two lost souls finally met. Laika, the loyal friend who had shared so many moments with Felipa in the landfill, was there to welcome her to the afterlife. Peace and serenity enveloped Felipa as she closed her eyes and smiled, freeing herself from the chains of the earthly world.

The scene was a painful and poetic contrast: life and death intertwined in a tragic ballet. The hearts of those who witnessed the outcome were filled with shock and sadness, but also with an understanding that Felipa's cycle of life had come to an end. Eternal peace had become her final destination.

Minutes passed like sighs amid the silence, broken only by the soft sobs of those present. In that place where violence and compassion had clashed, where hatred and love had collided, an aura of resignation and reflection remained. The story of the Virgin of the Dump and Pompeya left an indelible mark on the fabric of reality, reminding us of the inherent duality of humanity and the constant struggle between darkness and light.

Thus, in the stillness of the moment, two destinies intertwined and diverged simultaneously. Pompeya, trapped in her madness and despair, had met her own tragic end. Felipa, the Virgin of the Dump, had found the peace she longed for, uniting her spirit with that of her beloved Laika. And as the world continued to turn, their legacy would endure, reminding us that even in the darkest moments, kindness and compassion can shine with an intensity impossible to extinguish.

The white radiance that descended from the heavens seemed like a divine emanation bathing the Virgin of the Dump. It was a call to transcend earthly limitations and ascend to a higher plane of existence. Felipa, whose spirit had been a sun of hope and compassion, was destined to join the ranks of the beings of light. Higher laws, the same that govern celestial movements and universal energies, summoned her to a state of sanctity reserved for exceptional souls.

Responding to that celestial call, Felipa left behind the trappings of the material world and ascended, accompanied by her beloved Laika, to a realm beyond human comprehension. It was a fitting ending for her altruistic spirit, a culmination where her actions and sacrifices found their reward in an eternity of peace and love.

Meanwhile, Pompeya continued her tortuous journey in the darkness of madness. Her inner demons tormented her relentlessly, leading her to the deepest recesses of despair and pain. Trapped in a mental institution, her mind was a whirlwind of delusions and hallucinations, where the ghosts of her past haunted her relentlessly. Imaginary demons, personifications of her guilt and remorse, plagued her like ravenous creatures, tearing at her mind and plunging her into unbearable agony.

In their names and in their stories, an eternal lesson was preserved: the ability to choose the path of good or evil, compassion or envy, and how those choices, though seemingly small, could shape the destiny of an entire life. The tale of Felipa and Pompeya would become a constant echo in the consciousness of those who heard it, reminding them of the importance of choosing wisely and facing the consequences of their actions.